REVERE

THE SAINTHOOD – BOYS OF LOWELL HIGH BOOK 4

USA TODAY BESTSELLING AUTHOR

SIOBHAN DAVIS

Harlow Westbrook's life is the stuff of dreams. Married to her four soul mates and with a family she adores and a fulfilling career, she should be blissfully happy. Except she can't give Saint the one thing he craves—a biological child of his own. When cracks appear in their relationship, impacting the entire family unit, it threatens everything they have fought so hard for.

But Harlow has never been the type of woman to give up when things get tough.

Especially when her happily ever after is at stake.

PRAISE FOR THE SAINTHOOD SERIES

"Siobhan! Goodness. What have you done to me? *Resurrection* is freaking amazing! What a thrill ride with Harlow and her boys! I'm in love with them all!"

Ilsa Madden-Mills. Wall Street Journal bestselling author

"I devoured *Resurrection* in one sitting. It was sinfully sexy, dark, and taboo."

Ava Harrison. USA Today bestselling author

"*Resurrection* was the ultimate page-turner. I am addicted to Siobhan Davis's writing. Deliciously dark, I never wanted it to end."

Parker S. Huntington. USA Today bestselling author

"The only thing better than a Siobhan Davis book is a Siobhan Davis REVERSE HAREM book!!!"

S.E. Hall. NYT bestselling author

"Heart-stopping, intense, and hotter than hell! Siobhan Davis once again delivers an intriguing story with twists and turns you won't see coming. Five VENGEANCE IS HOT stars!"

K Webster. USA Today bestselling author

"You want this book in your life. No, you NEED it! Harlow is so fierce, and the Sainthood men are to die for. AMAZING!!"

Shantel Tessier. USA Today & WSJ bestselling author

Printed by Amazon
Paperback edition © August 2021

ISBN-13: 9798544085966

Originally published as part of The Sainthood: The Complete Series © November 2020
Valentine's Bonus Scene © February 2021
Editor: Kelly Hartigan (XterraWeb) editing.xterraweb.com
Cover design by Robin Harper wickedbydesigncovers.wixsite.com
Cover photo © www.depositphotos.com
Formatted by C.P. Smith

A NOTE FROM THE AUTHOR

This bonus novella was first published in the series box set. This book also contains a special Valentine's bonus scene, shared in Siobhan's Squad on Facebook, in February 2021.

This story is set twelve years after the epilogue in *Reign*.

I hope you enjoy catching up with the crew! Happy reading.

REVERE

THE SAINTHOOD – BOYS OF LOWELL HIGH BOOK 4

CHAPTER 1

Harlow

NUDGING THE FRONT door aside with my hip, I push into the house holding two overloaded grocery bags flush against my chest, praying I get to the kitchen before the kids realize I'm home and descend on me with the usual enthusiasm. I shut the door with my sneakered foot, wincing as it slams loudly behind me.

Shrieks ring out as I walk into the extended kitchen, and I spot Galen hunched over one of the rugrats beside the sink. The faucet is on, and Bishop is holding a wet cloth underneath the running water. Beads of water cling to my son's bare back, and he's wearing damp swim shorts, so I'm guessing they were out in the pool before the drama started. Depositing the groceries on the island unit, I step toward my husband. "What happened?" I ask, already knowing Aurora is involved. Our two-year old is a magnet for trouble, and she revels in it. If there's mischief involved, Rora will usually be at the center of it. God help us all when she's older.

Galen straightens up, and my lips twitch as my gaze roams over our youngest daughter. Rora is covered in flour, her olive-toned skin coated in a thick white downy layer. It even clings to her lashes and adheres to her long dark hair. "The kids were helping me bake chocolate chip cookies," Galen explains, leaning in to peck my lips. "I swear I only turned my back for two seconds, and Fireheart dumped the entire bag of flour over herself." He shakes his head, stifling a smile.

Crouching in front of my daughter, I gently brush flour off the lashes framing her warm brown eyes.

"I didn't mean to," she pouts, jutting her lip out. "Was an ax-dent." My heart swells at her cute little voice even though I know she's lying because dumping a bag of flour over her head is something our little Fireheart would do willingly and not by accident. But I find it hard to chastise her—unless she's being deliberately naughty—because she's curious about the world and desperate to know everything there is to know, and I never want to tame her excitement or stifle her exuberant personality.

"It will come off, and no one got hurt. That's the main thing." I smile as I tweak her flour-dusted nose.

"The flour goes in the bowl. Not over your head, stupid," Bishop says, rolling his eyes as he hands me the wet cloth.

"No name-calling, Bishop. Remember we talked about this." Galen sends our eldest a warning look that

2

would terrify most kids, but Bishop is no ordinary kid, and he takes *everything* in stride. He's like five going on fifty sometimes.

Rora glares at her big brother as I attempt to wipe the flour off her face. "You're mean."

"And you're naughty," Bishop retorts, blatantly ignoring Galen's words.

The flour on Rora's cheek turns to a gloopy paste as I gently scrub at her skin with the cloth. Fuck. I don't think this will wash off as easily as I initially thought. I picture screams and cries in my near future. Throwing the cloth in the sink, I decide I'm going to put her outside on the grass and try to shake as much of the flour off before hosing her down, and then I'll put her in the bath.

"Prodigy." Galen pins Bishop with a firmer look. "Be nice to your little sister, and leave the parenting to us." I worry about our son for a bunch of reasons; one being he's so serious sometimes. He has a natural tendency to take on responsibility that is way beyond his tender years. We had all assumed he was Theo's biological child until the test last year proved otherwise.

"Mommy." Luna slinks over to my side, draping her small body around me. She's wearing her *Frozen* terry-cloth poncho over a swimsuit. "Can you come in the pool?"

"I need to bathe Rora, put away the groceries, and make lunch. But I'll get in the pool after that." Gently tugging on one of her soft blonde curls, I smile at my gorgeous eldest daughter.

"Come on, princess." Galen pries Luna off me,

scooping her up into his arms. "Let's finish making the cookies, and then we'll go swimming." She beams at him, her jade-green eyes bright, her blonde curls bouncing as she snuggles into his chest. Luna is the most affectionate of our three kids. She's also the quietest. She breezed into this world four years ago with barely a whimper, and she hasn't caused us an ounce of trouble since.

Galen presses kisses into her hair, gazing adoringly at her, as he cradles her close. All my husbands are amazing fathers, and the way they love our kids is a thing of beauty. Watching these muscled, tatted, pierced men dote over our son and daughters makes my ovaries swoon, every damn time.

"Here, Mom." Bishop hands me a large beach towel. "Wrap Fireheart in that so she doesn't get flour all over the house."

"Don't call me that," Rora snaps, pouting again. "Only my daddies call me that." She plants her hands on her hips and thrusts her chest out, challenging her brother with her body language. It's priceless, and Galen and I share an amused look. "My name is *Aurora*," she tells her brother, as if he's unaware, enunciating her given name. Aurora has an amazing vocabulary for only two, and she never stops talking, chattering nonstop from the second she wakes every day until she conks out at night.

"Whatever." Bishop dismisses her with a shrug that enrages her. Her eyes narrow, and her nostrils flare as her temper rises.

I think the term "terrible twos" was coined for Aurora Sariah Westbrook, because neither of her siblings threw temper tantrums even close to the epic meltdowns we've witnessed with Rora. She must get that from me, because Caz is as easygoing as they come, and I can't imagine him as a little terror when he was younger. Mom says she sees the same determination and spirit in Rora and she reminds her of me as a kid. Maybe that's why I find it so hard to punish her when she's naughty. I never want to clip her wings. My parents enforced discipline in a way that also encouraged my true personality to shine, and I strive to be like that.

Quickly swaddling her in the towel, I bundle her into my arms before she launches herself at her brother. Those two are always arguing, but they are also each other's biggest defenders when anyone threatens or disrespects their sibling.

"Never a dull moment," Galen muses, leaning in to kiss me with Luna in his arms.

Our lips linger, and I wish we had time to get lost in one another. But spontaneous make-out sessions are a thing of the past since the kids came along. Between work and family life, we barely have time to breathe these days. Yet I wouldn't have it any other way. I love my life, and I wouldn't change anything.

Except for giving Saint the one thing he desperately desires. Something that has eluded us, so far.

"Gross," Bishop murmurs, watching us kiss. Rora wriggles in my arms, babbling away, while Luna giggles into Galen's neck.

"Kissing isn't gross," Galen says when we pull apart. "One day you'll find your own angel, and you'll want to kiss her, or him, nonstop until your lips fall off."

I arch a brow, an amused grin spreading across my mouth at his words.

"Ugh. Double gross," Bishop replies. "I'm never getting married."

"Why not?" I ask, repositioning the wriggly snake in my arms before I drop her.

"Because I'm gonna rule the world, and I'll be too busy for relationships."

I stare openmouthed at my son, momentarily speechless.

Galen's expression softens as he looks at him. "You can rule the world and have love in your life at the same time, Prodigy. Don't ever deny your heart the opportunity to love." Galen lifts his head, his intense green eyes locking on mine. "I almost did, and it nearly killed me."

I plant a soft kiss on his lips. "I love you."

I expect Bishop to emit another "gross" comment, but he's silent. Secretly, I know he loves how openly we all love one another. I grew up in a house where my parents were overtly affectionate, with each other and with me, and while I remember thinking similar "gross" thoughts as a kid, I also remember how much it warmed my heart to know my parents loved each other like that. It gave me an innate sense of security that couldn't be replicated after we lost Dad. I'm determined my kids grow up feeling that same sense of security and protectiveness. The kind that can only come from love. It's one of the reasons we shield nothing from our children. They know I am married to all their daddies, and they also know

Theo and Caz share a special kind of love too.

"I love you, too."

I will never tire of hearing those words from Galen or any of my husbands. I spent years believing I would never experience love, which makes what I share with my four guys even more special.

Rora huffs in exasperation, all out of patience, and Galen ruffles her hair. "Fireheart is restless. Go clean her up, and I'll start lunch after the cookies are in the oven."

"Thank you." I should protest because Galen has been with the kids all morning while I worked, so I'm sure he could use a break, but I don't because we're a team, and this way, everyone will be fed and back in the pool quicker. "I'll help when I'm done."

Besides, no one wants me in the kitchen. Some things definitely haven't changed. Galen and I are taking a cooking class downtown one night a week, and while his culinary skills have drastically improved, I still burn everything I touch. But I'm no quitter, and I'm not ready to throw in the towel just yet.

"You should relax," Bishop pipes up, moving over to the counter where the bowl and other cookie ingredients are set out. "You worked all morning. Let Daddy make lunch. I'll help."

"Daddy was working too." It's something I remind everyone of regularly. Galen chose to be a stay-at-home father, and it's no picnic. While the rest of us have jobs we can escape to, Galen doesn't have that luxury. He's around the kids, and this house, all the time. It's one of the reasons I asked him to take over managing the accounts for the fitness center I own and run. It's also one of the reasons I hired Jazz two years ago to help me manage the business so I can work part-time and be here to relieve Galen in the afternoons. Plus, I want to spend as much time as I can with the rugrats while they are small.

"I was trying to be diplomatic," Bishop says, and I quirk a brow. "Your cooking still sucks, Mom."

Galen chuckles, messing the top of Bishop's black hair. "Your diplomatic skills could use a little work."

"It's cool. And it's not like he's telling a lie. My talents lie outside of the kitchen," I quip, sending Galen a flirty look as I walk toward the double doors with my impatient daughter wriggling and mumbling in my arms.

"You'll never hear any complaints from me," he replies, fire blazing in his eyes, and I know his mind has gone to the same place as mine.

My core pulses with need, and I wonder if I can coax Theo out of his home office to watch the kids for a while after lunch so I can indulge in a quickie with Galen.

"You're perfect in all the ways that count."

I pin him with a sultry look, one that says, "you are so getting laid," conveying everything with the heat in my eyes, because I can't articulate those thoughts with innocent little eyes and ears around.

Galen's eyes darken with sheer lust, and I rush out of the room, desperate to bathe my daughter and get lunch over and done with so I can put my sexy plan into action.

CHAPTER 2

Harlow

"POPS!" RORA RACES across the hardwood floor of Theo's office, making a beeline for my husband. I lounge against the doorway, hoping we haven't interrupted him in the middle of something important.

Last year, Diesel promoted Theo to head of the information and technology department within VERO. It was a massive promotion. One he thoroughly deserved, and I couldn't be prouder of all he's achieved. The only downside is he now has to work out of their Washington, D.C. headquarters building at least two to three days a week. It's too far to drive on a daily basis and too expensive to use private jets to fly him to and from HQ each day, so Theo flies business class to D.C. on Tuesdays, returning home on Thursday nights.

We bought a penthouse apartment in the city so at

least he has some place to call home while he's there. On the odd occasion, I've gone to D.C. with him. I enjoy exploring the city during the day while he works and basking in his undivided attention at night. But I don't like being away from the kids for long, so I've only done it a couple of times. Caz keeps him company sometimes as well, and the kids are used to all of us coming and going at different times.

We built on at the back of the house last year, after Theo got his promotion, extending the kitchen-slash-dining room, adding a playroom for the kids, and a second home office for Theo. The original office is shared between the rest of us because we largely spend our days at our respective businesses, yet we still need a place to do some additional work from home. And Galen takes care of the accounts for my fitness center and the two garages Saint and Caz jointly own, so he needed space to work from home.

Theo removes the headphones from his ears, setting them down on the desk before swiveling in his chair. Rora barrels into him, and he lifts her, throwing her up into the air.

Her giggles reverberate throughout the room. "Again, Pops!"

He buries his head in her hair, hugging her little body tight to his chest. "Why do you smell like you've just had a bath?" he asks, standing.

"Because I just did, silly," she says, like it's normal to have a bath in the middle of the day, during the height of summer when most days are spent in and out of the pool.

He tosses her up high in the air. Her squeals tickle my eardrums, and I smile. "It sounds like someone was up to mischief." Theo waggles his brows, and she bats her eyelashes, flashing him the biggest, most innocent smile, looking like butter wouldn't melt in her mouth.

"Someone decided it would be fun to dump a bag of flour over her head," I explain, pushing off the doorway and walking toward them. Though I doubt she'll do it again. Not after the ordeal we just endured trying to get it all out.

"Fireheart." Theo shakes his head, but he's smiling. "What are we going to do with you? Hmm?" He kisses her cheek.

"Love me?" Rora says, batting her eyelashes, and I choke on a laugh.

The adoring look Theo gives her melts every part of me. "You are already loved, Rora." He dots kisses all over her face. "So, so much."

"I love you too, Pops." Miraculously, she snuggles into the crook of his neck, snaking her chubby arms around his neck. They have a special bond, and I know how much it pleases Caz that his biological daughter is particularly drawn to his lover.

"Any of that lovin' left to go around?" I joke as I come up in front of them.

"Always plenty of love for my wife," Theo says, opening his arm and pulling me into their embrace. We kiss, and a soft palm adheres to my cheek.

"When I gwo up, I'm gonna be just like Mommy," Rora says. "I'm gonna have lots and lots of hu-bands."

We break apart, and I smile at my daughter. "I hope you are as lucky as me." Theo and I exchange a look, and in his hazel eyes I see the boy I have loved since I was fourteen. I tuck his hair behind one ear, marveling at how young he still looks. It's like he hasn't changed at all. He still wears his hair to the base of his neck, despite the shade they throw at him at VERO HQ, and he still has the same toned lean build. The others work out religiously in the gym, but apart from a daily swim, Theo is content with his slighter build.

"We might need to put a limit on that number," Theo murmurs, carefully setting Rora on the ground, as his arm tightens around my waist and he pulls me in closer to his side. "I have a feeling Saintly will struggle to deal with even one."

"You're not wrong," I agree, watching Rora grab hold of Theo's hand. "He's already so protective of both of them." I glance over my shoulder at his desk. "Can you join us for lunch, or are we interrupting?"

Theo presses a kiss to my temple. "I always have time for family lunch. I've got thirty minutes before my next con call."

"C'mon then, Pops." Rora tugs on his hand, dragging him forward.

"How was work?" Theo asks as we walk out of his office side by side.

"Busy. And the waiting list is growing by the day. Jazz and I met with an architect and a representative from a construction company this morning to discuss plans to extend."

When I graduated from Brown, I leased a building in Providence and set up my fitness center. It's no ordinary fitness center. For starters, it's for women only. And as well as the usual fitness classes and standard gym, we offer self-defense classes and boxing, and we have a small shooting range out back. Recently, we partnered with a local sexual assault charity to offer support services to their members.

Four years ago, when the lease on the building went up for sale, I purchased it so I could do what I like with the property. Hence why my comanager—Jazz—and I set up the meeting today. If we add more square footage, we can accept more new members. "I hate turning anyone down. Not when they need it."

I fully believe self-defense should be on the curriculum, as a general class, within schools, but until that happens, I am doing all I can to prepare young girls to cope in a world that is growing increasingly violent. A couple of times a year, I speak at local schools and colleges about the importance of self-defense and how important it is to be able to protect yourself in our current society. As soon as my girls are old enough, I'll be teaching them everything I know.

"Are you going to go ahead with it?" Theo asks as we enter the kitchen.

"I hope so, but I need Galen to crunch the numbers for me first." The business part of my brain says it would be unintelligent to expand if the cost isn't covered by forecasted new memberships, but the compassionate part says screw the money. We can afford to take a hit. We are lucky we are comfortable with plenty of money. We still haven't used much out of my inheritance, and while Galen dipped into his savings to build us a vacation home on the grounds of his old home back in Prestwick, he has plenty left over. Theo's high salary more than covers our entire living expenses so the money the rest of us brings in mainly goes into our savings account.

I feel so fortunate, which is why it really doesn't matter what Galen's financial analysis unearths. I'm expanding even if it means we lose money on the build.

"Let's not pretend anything I show you will make a difference," Galen says, handing a bowl of salad to Bishop. "You're going to do it regardless."

"You're right. I am." I love how well he knows me. How well they all know me. "I don't care about the money. I want to help as many girls and women as I can. That's the only thing that matters."

Rora lets go of Theo's hand, looping her arm through Luna's as they head outdoors. I glance through the open double doors, seeing Galen has set the table outside for lunch al fresco. My favorite.

"I'm proud of you," Theo says, reeling me into his arms.

"We all are," Galen says, coming up behind me. He brushes my dark hair to one side, dusting kisses against my neck.

Theo smothers my lustful groan with his hot mouth, and I cling to his arms as Galen holds my hips from behind. Theo is the first to break our embrace. "We better stop before we reach the point of no return."

"Spoilsport." I fake pout even though I know he's right.

"I need you, angel," Galen says against my ear. "It's been too long. Saintly can fuck off if he thinks he's hogging you tonight. I'm calling dibs."

"I was planning on asking Theo to watch the kids so we could have a quickie," I say, craning my head back, watching Galen's eyes light up. "But he has a con call."

"I can watch them after my call," Theo offers. "If you make it worth *my* while," he adds, flashing me a wicked grin.

Every nerve ending sparks to life in my body as I turn to face him. I can't remember the last time we had sexy time during the day, and I need zero convincing. I plant my hands on his hard chest, pressing my body against his. "Trust me, I'll make it worth your while."

Theo grins. "Then we have a deal."

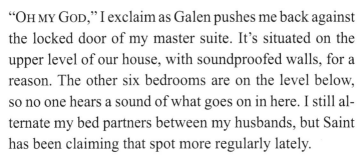

"OH MY GOD," I exclaim as Galen pushes me back against the locked door of my master suite. It's situated on the upper level of our house, with soundproofed walls, for a reason. The other six bedrooms are on the level below, so no one hears a sound of what goes on in here. I still alternate my bed partners between my husbands, but Saint has been claiming that spot more regularly lately.

I try not to think about the reasons for that as Galen's mouth descends on mine, because he deserves my full attention. His hands are desperate, his lips greedy, as he brutalizes my mouth while ripping my yoga pants and panties down my legs. I yank his running shorts down over his hips, freeing his monster cock and licking my lips.

"Need you now, angel," he says, lifting me by the waist and positioning his length against my entrance.

"Wait!" I shriek when I feel him nudging against me. "Condom." His heavy sigh says it all. "Galen."

Slowly, he lowers me to my feet, bending down to fully remove his shorts. "It's okay. I get it, and I want this for Saint. For both of you, but I fucking hate wearing condoms again. I miss being inside you with no barrier."

"It won't be forever." *I hope.* Because things aren't exactly going according to plan. I remove my sneakers and kick my yoga pants away as Galen strides to the bedside table where I keep our sex toys and supplies stash.

"It's fine. I'm being selfish." He removes a foil packet from the drawer.

I pull my top off over my head as I walk toward the bed. "It's natural to be selfish, and I know you love your cousin."

"I do." He whips his top off, letting it join the rest of our clothes on the floor. "And I love you." Unsnapping my bra, he flings it aside, and a shudder works its way through me as he palms my breasts in his large hands, his fingers flicking my nipples until they are hardened peaks. "So fucking much." His lips claim mine in a softer kiss this time, and I cling to him as he explores my mouth with his tongue. When he pushes me down flat on the bed, I spread my legs, anticipation building as he crawls over me.

He kneels, rolling the condom over his length. "I wish I had time to worship you. To go slow."

"But we both know the kids won't give us long before they come looking for us. Even with Theo entertaining them," I say, flattening my hands on his chiseled abs as he lines up his cock at my pussy. "Besides, hard and fast is our thing, so fuck my brains out, Galen. Remind me of all the reasons why I'm yours."

And he does. Meeting my demand with every powerful surge of his hips as he thrusts inside me, over and over again.

THE SAINTHOOD

CHAPTER 3

Harlow

"DAMN IT," THEO HISSES, when an incoming call flashes on the screen of his laptop, as I kneel between his bare legs underneath the desk. His shorts are pooled at his ankles, his thighs spread wide, and my mouth hovers over his erect cock, ready to reward him for taking babysitting duty so I could fuck Galen. "I've got to take this," he says over a resigned sigh.

My fingers curl around his throbbing length. "So take it." I flash him a devilish grin. "I can be quiet."

He stares at me as I slowly start pumping him in my hand, and I see the conflict on his face. The professional in him doesn't want to take this phone call while I'm pleasuring him, but he's horny and primed to explode, and he needs this.

"Answer it," I demand, taking the decision out of his

hands.

He presses a button on the side of his earpiece. "Diesel. What's up?"

Oh, this just got a whole lot more interesting. Screw toning it down. I am *so* having my fun with this.

My tongue darts out, swiping the crown of Theo's cock, and he jolts in the chair, eyes widening as he cautions me with a warning look. Ignoring him, I lower my lips over his warm length, grazing my teeth against his velvety-soft skin as I move up and down his erection.

"Uh-huh," he croaks, his hips automatically thrusting into my mouth as I suck him deeper. "I, ah, sent you that report last night. Didn't you get it?"

I quicken my pace, pulling the skin on his dick taut as my fingers curl around the base of his shaft and I pump him with my hand as my mouth works him over nice and good.

"I'll resend it," he all but shouts as I suction my lips hard against his length. "I'm fine," he adds after a couple of beats, shooting me with another loaded look, which I ignore. His eyes roll back in his head as I take him to the back of my throat, stretching my mouth wide to take all of him. "Yes. Sure," he pants as I purposely make a loud slurping sound.

He makes a slicing motion with his hand against his throat, warning me to cut it out, but this is the most fun I've had in ages, and I'm not about to stop now. I pretend to behave, fixing him with a fake obedient look as my lips move quietly up and down his length, and the fear on his face drops a few notches.

He nods his head as he listens to whatever Diesel is saying, closing his eyes briefly as he instinctively spreads his thighs a little wider. With my free hand, I quickly uncap the lube, coating my index finger in the liquid. "I can take a look into that. How—" A strangled sound rips from his mouth when I shove my finger into his ass, pumping it in and out as I glide my mouth up and down his length with renewed purpose. I make loud slurping noises, adding a few moans and groans for extra effect, stifling the laughter bubbling beneath the surface of my chest when I spot the horrified look on Theo's face. There is no way Diesel doesn't know what's going down now. Ha!

Theo's balls tighten, his cock straining as precum leaks from the tip, and I sense he's close. He knows he can't stop this, and I think he could happily murder me right now—even if I am the cause of his imminent pleasure.

"I, ah." He groans into the phone, and I push my finger up farther in his ass until I feel his prostate. "I'll call you back," he roars into the phone, seconds before he detonates in my mouth, shooting ropes of salty cum down my throat. His hips jerk as he empties his seed in my mouth, and I can't keep the grin off my face. His dick makes a popping sound as I finally release him, sitting back on my ankles, waiting to be reprimanded.

"You." He pulls me up onto his lap. "Are going to pay for that." He nips at my earlobe, tugging on it. "Such a naughty, naughty girl." He cups my already damp crotch through my yoga pants. "Diesel totally knows what you were doing."

I arch a brow. "That was the point."

"I'm supposed to be a professional." He pushes the heel of his hand into my crotch, rubbing me through the material of my clothes.

I squirm on his lap, wrapping my arms around his neck. "You *are* a professional. Me blowing you while you're working doesn't change that fact."

"I'd rather my boss didn't know the details of my sex life." He narrows his eyes as he continues teasing my pussy.

"It's not like he's a saint. I happen to know, for a fact, he regularly fucks Denise in his office. On the desk, against the windows, on top of—"

He clamps his hand over my mouth. "TMI, babe." I snicker. "At least now I know what you ladies talk about when you're together."

Diesel married Denise six years ago and they have twin three-year-old daughters. I warmed to her instantly, and we're good friends. Even though we don't have much time to meet in person—what with her living in D.C.—we talk weekly by phone. She knows all about my history with Diesel, and it never fazed her that we slept together in the past. She's good people.

"Sex, sex, and more sex," I joke, leaning down to kiss him.

"I love tasting my cum on your tongue," he murmurs against my lips as his hand breaches the band on my pants, sliding underneath my panties. A whimper escapes my mouth as his fingers part my folds, and he slides two digits inside my wet warmth. "But not as much as I love tasting *your* cum on *my* tongue."

I shriek as he lifts me off him, yanks my pants and panties down, and sets me against the edge of the desk.

"Spread 'em, queenie," he commands, his eyes darkening with lust as his gaze zeros in on my bare pussy.

I do as I'm told, parting my thighs and gripping the edge of the desk as his hot tongue flattens against my clit, and it's not long before I'm falling apart again.

***

"Honey, I'm home!" Caz calls out a few hours later as I'm setting the table for dinner. Theo is helping Galen in the kitchen, and the kids are plonked in front of the TV watching cartoons.

"Hey, queenie," my giant teddy bear of a husband says as he enters the room. "Miss me?" he asks before lifting me up and swinging me around. I giggle. Caz has the same routine every day when he and Saint return from work, and I love it, finding familiarity in his words and the comfort of knowing I get a warm embrace every day. Placing my feet on the ground, he bundles me into a hug. "Heads-up," he whispers in my ear. "He hasn't forgotten what time of the month it is. He's on a mission."

I hate how my good mood plummets at his words and how guilty I feel for my natural reaction. Things are becoming complicated the longer this goes on.

Saint stomps into the room, and it's as if his presence sucks all the oxygen from the air. Or perhaps it's only me who feels like that.

"Dad!" Luna appears at the door from the playroom, her pretty little face lighting up the second she sees Saint.

"Princess." Saint drops to one knee, opening his arms. "Come give me some loving." He waggles his brows, and she giggles, racing across the kitchen and flinging herself into his arms. Tears prick my eyes as I watch him hug Luna, his eyes closing and chest heaving with emotion as he holds her close.

I know how much Saint loves all the kids, and he shares a special closeness with Luna. But I also know he's hugging her and imagining she's his own flesh and blood. Wishing she shared his DNA because he is desperate for a child of his own. He has never voiced those words to me. I expect he has never voiced those words to the others either. I don't know for sure because we skate around the issues, which is not usual for us. Open communication has been the cornerstone of our relationship from the very start, but this is different. We're in uncharted territory, and I don't think any of us know how to navigate it. I don't want to upset Saint. He doesn't want to upset me. And the others don't want to upset either one of us.

I'm terrified it's going to destroy what we've built here. I already feel cracks forming, and I don't know how to fix it. If only I would get pregnant, but we've been trying for eight months with no success.

"Miss me?" Saint asks Luna, and she nods, snuggling into his chest.

"We made cookies," Rora says, ambling into the

kitchen followed by Bishop.

"Chocolate chip?" Caz asks, scooping his wild daughter into his arms.

"Poppa Bear!" Rora giggles as Caz tickles her. "That tickles!"

"That's because I'm the Tickle Monster," Caz says, chuckling as he continues tormenting her. Rora squeals, her loud laughter bouncing off the walls, helping to loosen the edge off my stress.

Saint releases Luna, standing. "How long until dinner?" he asks Galen.

"Twenty minutes."

Saint grabs my hand. "That's enough time."

"We can wait till later," I say, really not in the mood.

"Queenie." He pulls me in close, pressing his warm mouth to my ear. "You're ovulating, and we don't have a minute to waste. Some experts say you only have twelve hours to fertilize the egg. Every second we wait is a wasted opportunity."

Saint is like an encyclopedia on fertilization and reproduction. At first, I thought it was cute. Now, I wish he'd drop it. The more he pushes the agenda, the more stressed I feel. It's even gotten to the stage where I've begun to dread sex with him.

And I love sex. That hasn't changed.

Nor has the fact I love Saint with my entire being.

I want to make him happy. I want to give him a biological child. But I feel like I'm failing him because it just isn't happening, and he's getting angrier while I'm growing more miserable.

"Start without us if we're not back," Saint says, hell-bent on fucking me.

"Surely, it can wait until after," Theo interjects, his troubled gaze flitting to mine.

"Butt out, man." Saint clings to my hand as he warns Theo to mind his own business. He is wound up so tight, and I hate I'm the cause of it.

"It's fine," I say, wanting to defuse the rapidly growing tension. "Let's go." I tug on Saint's hand, just wanting to get this over and done with now.

"THE TIMING FEELS right," Saint says a few minutes later as he thrusts inside me. "It's going to happen this month." He hovers over me on my bed, staring at me as he fucks me, but it's like he's looking through me. He's not really here with me in this moment. He's on a mission—the goal to knock me up, and that is all he can see these days. He's obsessed with impregnating me, and it's like he's lost sight of everything else that is important.

I offer him a weak smile because I'm afraid if I try to speak the tears I'm holding at bay will erupt like a volcano.

He slams into me violently, pounding as deep as he can go, a look of fierce concentration on his face. He holds my hips in place with his firm hands, keeping me steady, as he rams his cock inside me, thrusting inside me over and over again until he roars out his release, collapsing on top of me. A sneaky tear leaks out of the corner of one eye, but I swipe it away before he notices.

He rolls onto his side, his chest heaving. His fingers glide down my body, pressing against my clit. I jerk, pulling away from him, swinging my legs over the other side of the bed. "We need to get up," I say with my back to him. "Dinner is getting cold."

"You didn't come," he says, his voice flat and devoid of emotion.

I'm surprised he noticed. Sex with him has become robotic, and I hate it. He barely even kisses me anymore because I can't get pregnant from kisses. It's like all he cares about is putting a baby in my belly, and he doesn't see how much he's hurting me. How distant we have become, even though he fucks me way more than the others. I don't know how much longer I can keep doing this. Now, I don't even want him to touch me. "I came earlier with Theo and Galen. I'm fine," I say, in an equally monotone voice.

"Good," he says, sounding like he doesn't mean it. "But you should go again. Pregnancy is more likely if the woman orgasms during sex."

"News flash," I grit out, glaring at him over my shoulder. "We already had sex, and I didn't come during the act, so just drop it."

"Fine," he snaps, grabbing one of the pillows. "At least lie back so I can put this under your hips."

"What?" I splutter because this is new.

"I read an article today that said if you stay still after sex, with your hips propped up, that my sperm has a better chance of reaching your egg."

His comment would be funny if the situation wasn't so heartbreaking. Anger prickles under the surface of my skin, and I'm close to telling him to fuck off. Until I see the look on his face, and I stuff the words back down. Underneath the anger and frustration on his handsome face lies vulnerability and devastation. He's in too much pain to shield it from me, and I can't deny him, even if it sounds like an old wives' tale and it seems like it won't make a bit of difference.

I can do this for him.

I lie back on the bed and let him place the pillow under my hips. He lies down beside me, both of us flat on our backs, staring silently at the ceiling. I close my eyes, hating this. Hating that I can't talk to him. That I'm afraid of saying the wrong thing. Fearful I will take the conversation to a place he might not have gone yet. I've gotten pregnant easily all the other times, with little effort, so I have wondered if the reason I'm not getting pregnant this time is down to an issue with Saint. I hate myself for even thinking it, but if we don't get pregnant soon, the next logical step will be to investigate why. What if he has a low sperm count or some other issue? That will destroy him. Which is why I can't even broach the topic with him.

"Time's up," he says, and the bed moves as he climbs off it.

I blink my eyes open and sit up, leaning back against the headboard. A tight pain slices across my chest, and my thoughts are heavy as I watch him get dressed.

"I'll meet you downstairs." He walks off without

another word, and I give myself a silent pep talk, willing myself to get moving instead of giving in to the need to curl into a ball and cry myself to sleep.

Somehow, I get up, get dressed, and make my way downstairs. Dinner is already in mid-flow, the kids bantering with their dads, when I walk into the room. Galen hops up, walking to the stove to retrieve my dinner. "I've got it," I say, appearing beside him. "Don't let your dinner go cold." He takes one look at me and frowns. Glancing quickly over his shoulder, he puts the plate down on the counter, sliding his arm around my waist. "Are you okay?" he asks, lowering his tone.

"I'm fine." I flash him a fake smile, and his frown deepens.

"Do you want me to talk to him?"

Tears stab the backs of my eyes. He knows. Maybe they all do. I shake my head, forcing my tears to subside. "Don't get involved. This is between us."

He looks like he wants to argue but thinks better of it. "Come on. Let's get some food into you."

I let Galen lead me to the table, pull out my chair, and set my dinner on the table in front of me. Lifting my silverware, as if on autopilot, I force food down my tight throat, listening to the chatter and laughter around the table as if I'm a bystander.

After, I lie, telling them I have a migraine, letting them fuss over me before I'm sent to bed, pretending I don't see the anger on Saint's face or feel the flood of relief as I curl up in bed alone, crying myself to sleep.

THE SAINTHOOD

CHAPTER 4

Harlow

"I COME BEARING gifts," Jazz says the following day, stepping into my office uninvited. She waves a paper bag at me. "Lunch from the deli."

"I thought you were teaching a class?" I ask, looking up from my laptop. While we run the business and leave most of the classes to the trainers we hire, we both make a point of teaching a couple of classes a week, for no other reason than we enjoy it.

"I got Monica to cover for me. You looked like you could use food and a talk." She closes the door and walks to my desk.

"I'm that obvious?" I ask, putting my pen down.

"I'm your bestie." She places a bag down in front of me before taking a seat across from me. "It's my job to notice when you're upset. What's wrong?" She opens her own bag, extracting a wrap, an apple, and a bottle of water.

I hired Jazz four years ago, just after I bought the building. At first, we were just coworkers, but over time we've become the best of friends. I don't trust easily, and I've never been the kind of woman who has tons of friends. I had girls I hung out with in college, but I never called any of them friends, and I don't see any of them or keep in contact with them anymore. They were mere acquaintances. That's all. I find it hard to relate to other women sometimes. In part, because my lifestyle is different than most and there is a lot of prejudice, judgment, and jealousy from other women when they discover I'm in a polyamorous relationship. Also, I was married and not interested in attending parties or hooking up with frat boys so that set me apart from other college students.

Diesel's Denise was the first woman since Sariah that I could call a good friend. Until Jazz. But even though I'm close with both Denise and Jazz, I haven't confided in either of them about this, and I'm not sure what that says about me. Maybe no one will ever replace Sariah in my life, because if she were still alive, there is no doubt I would've confided in her immediately.

"Lo." Jazz reaches across the desk to grab my hand. Her eyes are full of compassion. "You can tell me anything. You know that. I will never judge you or betray your confidence."

"I know that." The words feel choked over the lump in my throat.

"Is it Bishop?" she asks, squeezing my hand. "Is he sick again?"

I shake my head. "No, thank God. He's doing much better since the operation, and Galen and I took him to the cardiologist for a checkup last week. Everything looks good."

Last year, Bishop collapsed at kindergarten and had to be rushed to the emergency room. We discovered he had a congenital heart defect, one that had gone undiagnosed since birth. He had an operation to repair the small hole in his heart, and his doctor has told us he should live a long, healthy, and happy life. He will have to be monitored frequently, but as long as he is taking care of himself and getting regular checkups, there shouldn't be any reason to worry.

God knows we all did enough of that last year. We were terrified.

"Is it Galen then? Does he still feel guilty?"

I squeeze her hand before withdrawing mine, opening my bag, and removing my lunch as I speak. "Even though he's processed everything that happened with Bishop and come out the other side, I think Galen will always feel guilty," Galen was in bad shape during that time. He was worried for Bishop, and the situation brought buried memories to the surface. For him, it was a lot like watching helplessly as his sister suffered. Even after Bishop recovered, and we knew he was going to be fine, Galen frequently woke from nightmares. I spent a lot of nights comforting him in the early hours, and we spent hours upon hours talking about it until he worked through his feelings.

"While his sister Mya had a different heart condition," I continue, "there is nothing any of us can say to make him agree it's not his fault. He will always carry that, but at least he has found a way to live again. He was depressed and scared for so long." I pause for a moment, remembering how worried about him we all were. But Galen is tough, and he has made his peace with it now. "The doctors can't even say for sure if it's genetic. It could be coincidental that Bishop had a heart condition and so did his aunt. The most important thing is, he is healthy and well. It hasn't scared him or altered him in any of the ways that count."

"So, what *is* troubling you?"

I decide to fess up—if I don't talk to someone about it, I'm likely to fall apart. More than that, I need her advice on what to do. I take a sip of my water, and she takes a bite out of her wrap as she waits patiently for me to explain. "When I first got pregnant, we made a joint decision not to find out who the biological father was. It was the same when Luna and Aurora came along. It doesn't matter whose DNA flows in their veins because they are all of our children. Every one of my husbands is an amazing father, and everything was fine until Bishop got sick, and it forced us to relook at things." My heart is heavy as I recall one of the more difficult times of my life. I take a bite of my wrap as I grapple with my emotions.

"In what way? Did you need to know for a blood transfusion or something?"

"It was more that we realized we needed to know in case there were other genetic issues we needed to be aware of."

"Like Caz's mom having Parkinson's."

I nod. "Exactly." We found out about Mrs. Evans just after Bishop was diagnosed and it was a no-brainer by then. We won't take risks with our kids' lives, and it's better to know the full familial history so we are prepared for any future situations.

"I still don't understand what the issue is," Jazz says, biting into her apple.

I take another sip of water, before slouching in my chair. I flip the bottle cap between my fingers as I get to the heart of the matter. "The paternity tests revealed Galen is Bishop's bio dad, Theo is Luna's bio dad, and Caz is Rora's."

Awareness sparks to life in her eyes. "Saint is upset none of them are his."

I bob my head. "Out of all my husbands, Saint has always been the most possessive, the most alpha. The instant we got the results, I knew he'd feel left out. That he'd want to rectify the situation."

"Don't you want any more kids?"

I straighten up, leaning my elbows on the table. "Honestly, I'd have a football field full of kids. I love babies. I adore my children. That's not it." I gulp over the pained lump in my throat. "We've been trying for eight months, and I'm still not pregnant."

Her features soften. "That's not too long. Especially when you've given birth to three kids within four years.

Your body probably needs some time to recover before it's ready to go again."

"That could be true, but Saint is a man on a mission, and it's taking over everything." Pain slices across my chest. "He's obsessed, Jazz. He knows my cycle better than I know it myself. He's read every book he can get his hands on. He practically forces vitamins and health smoothies down my throat. I'm afraid to indulge in snacks because I see the look he gives me if I dare put anything unhealthy into my body. He makes the others use condoms so I don't accidentally get pregnant by them, and he actually suggested last week that I should abstain from sex with my other husbands so my body is less tired and more ready for him. He's starting to sound legit crazy. He's unpredictable and erratic, and sometimes, when he's fucking me, he seems angry, as if he hates me." A sob rips from my chest, and I hang my head, my body shaking as deep-seated anguish races through me.

"Oh, Harlow." She reaches out, taking my hand again. "Why didn't you tell me any of this before?"

I lift my head, looking her in the face. "Saint is a proud guy, and he didn't want anyone to know. He asked me not to mention it to you or Denise, and I didn't want to go against his wishes."

"I understand, and I'm not mad. I'm just upset you've been dealing with this alone. I should've been there for you."

"I don't know what to do, and it's getting worse." Tears are dripping down my face, and I'm powerless to stop them. "I have loved sex from the minute I became sexually active, but I'm starting to dread sex with Saint because it's not enjoyable anymore. He's all cold and clinical." My sobs pick up in earnest, and she rounds the desk, wrapping her arms around me. "He came home last night, and he didn't even say hello to me. It was all "you're ovulating, we need to fuck," and I actually flinched when he tried to touch me after the deed was done."

My lower lip wobbles as I peer into her face. "I'm terrified this is taking over our lives and ruining what I have with him. And if that happens, it will ruin the whole family dynamic. Worse, what if I can't get pregnant? What if I can't give him the child he so desperately desires? I'll feel like a failure, and I don't know if he'll ever be able to forgive me."

"It might not be your fault, Lo. Have you considered that maybe the issue is with Saint? Maybe you should both get tested."

My chest heaves painfully. "I have considered that, but it would only make things worse. I'd rather I was the failure than Saint thinking it's him. If he can't father children, it will devastate him, Jazz." I swallow over the anguished lump in my throat. "If it was anyone but Saint, they'd deal with it. But Saint won't handle it well. I know he won't. He…"

I bury my head in my hands, full-on sobbing, while Jazz hugs me, rubbing a soothing hand up and down my back. "It's going to be okay, Lo."

"I wish I could believe that," I rasp, looking at her

through blurry eyes.

"You have had three healthy babies. You're still young, and you have plenty of time to get pregnant. Even if there are any issues, there are so many options nowadays. You *will* have another baby. I feel it in my bones." She bites on the corner of her lip. "Do you want to know what I think?"

"Always." I nod, sniffling, accepting the tissue she hands to me.

"I think all this stress is stopping you from getting pregnant. I'm no doctor, but this can't be helping."

"I think you're right, but how do I handle this? I'm afraid to say any of this to Saint because I don't want to hurt his feelings. And I can't talk to the others because it's not fair to put them in the middle of this."

She wipes moisture off my cheeks. "I'm surprised you haven't spoken to them because communication has always been key in your relationship. I've envied you that. You can ask Ken. He'll tell you I've told him our marriage needs to be built on open communication like yours."

"This is different."

"It is." She returns to her seat, handing me another tissue. "This is when communication is even more important. You love Saint and he loves you. He wants a baby with you, and you want a baby with him. You both want the same thing. It's the way you are going about it that's all wrong, and if you don't speak up now, irreparable damage may be caused to your relationship."

She is not telling me anything I don't know, but

hearing Jazz say it gives me the confidence boost I've been lacking. I'm Harlow fucking Westbrook, and I don't run from anything. Especially not from difficult conversations with one of the men I love. And I never lie down and accept defeat. Determination zips through my veins, and I blot the last of my tears from my eyes, the first hint of a genuine smile appearing on my lips. "You're right, and I needed you to tell me that." I get up, and Jazz stands. I pull her into a hug. "Thank you."

"It's going to be okay, Harlow. I just know it is. Get your relationship with Saint back on track. Remove the pressure, and everything will happen naturally, I bet."

"Can you handle things if I take off?" There is no time like the present. None of the guys are working today, and I know they will either be in the pool or at our private beach with the kids, so it's the perfect time to pull Saint aside for a private conversation.

"Go. I've got things here."

I hug her again. "I owe you."

"Any time. You did the same for me when Ken and I hit that rough patch."

"That's what friends are for."

"Truth, sister." She releases me with a smile. "Call me later, and let me know how it goes."

"I will," I say, grabbing my purse as I exit my office, feeling less burdened than I did when I arrived at work today.

THE SAINTHOOD

CHAPTER 5

Saint

"WHERE ARE THE kids?" I ask when I return from the gym, finding the house eerily quiet. Lo is working, but the guys aren't, so the place should be messy and noisy, and it's not. I step out onto the patio where Galen, Theo, and Caz are currently lounging by the pool.

"Freya took them out for ice cream." Freya is one of the neighbor's kids. She's sixteen and she recently began babysitting for us, but we generally only hire her at night, when we're taking Lo out to dinner, so this is unusual.

I dump my gym bag on the ground, running a hand through my freshly-washed hair. "Is there a reason we needed to offload the rugrats?"

The guys trade looks, and I'm instantly on guard.

"Yeah." Galen stands. "We need to talk to you, and we didn't want the kids around."

My hackles are instantly raised, and I fold my arms across my chest, leveling them with a dark look. "You know how I feel about being ambushed," I snarl.

"And you know how we feel about Lo," Theo coolly replies, rising to stand beside Galen.

"Let's talk inside," Caz says. "We don't want anything carrying on the wind."

I follow them inside, my heart heavy with the knowledge of what's about to be said. For the first time in a long time, I find myself in isolation, and it's not a good place to be. Theo and Caz drop down on one of the couches in the living room while Galen flops onto the other one. I stand, crossing my arms over my chest again, bracing myself for it.

"Sit down, man," Galen says.

"I'd rather stand."

"We just want to talk this out like civilized adults," Theo says. "There's no need to raise proverbial fists. We're family, and we need to discuss this. Just sit down and relax."

"That's not how we roll," Caz adds. "It seems we've all forgotten that."

Reluctantly, I sit down, still eyeing them warily. "I know what you're going to say, and you shouldn't get involved. This is between Lo and me."

Galen sits up straighter. "That's bullshit, and you know it. This affects all of us, and it's gone on too long. You're being a dick, and if you don't stop hurting her, we have a big problem."

I clench my fists into balls. "I know things are a little

strained, but you can't accuse me of hurting her. I would *never* hurt her. You all know that."

"We know it's not intentional," Theo says, always the peacemaker. "But you *are* hurting her, Saint. We all see it."

I drag a hand through my hair. "You don't understand because it wasn't like this for any of you. She got pregnant like that all the previous times"—I snap my fingers—"and we weren't concerned with who the father was, because it didn't matter back then."

"Does it really matter now?" Caz asks, softening his tone as he leans his elbows on his knees. "The kids adore you, man. Who cares which blood flows through their veins? They are ours in all the ways that count. We are all Westbrooks."

"It matters to me. *I* fucking care." I thump a hand over my heart, swallowing thickly over the painful lump in my throat. "I love Bishop, Luna, and Rora with my whole heart, but I want my own kid with Lo. Are you telling me you wouldn't feel the same way in my shoes?"

The silence is deafening.

"Exactly." I slump back on the couch.

"We don't know how we would feel," Galen says, his face radiating compassion. "Perhaps we would feel how you feel, but I'd like to think you'd intervene if you saw me obsessing and hurting our wife in the process."

"What the actual fuck?" I roar, throwing my hands in the air. I know I might have gone a tad bit overboard, but throwing that shit at me isn't cool. "I'm not *obsessing*. I've been educating myself so I'm well informed. So we have every chance to conceive. I don't want Lo to feel like it's all on her, so I'm sharing the responsibility."

"You're taking it too far," Caz says. "You're losing sight of what's important in your quest to knock her up."

I jump to my feet. "Who fucking died and made you the expert?" I jab my finger in Caz's direction. "You don't get to dictate to me about this."

"I fucking do when you're stressing our wife out and upsetting her," he replies, climbing to his feet and glaring at me.

"Everyone, calm down." Theo stands, his gaze bouncing between us. "We'll get nowhere if this continues."

"If Lo's so upset, why hasn't she come to me?"

"Because I was afraid of hurting you," she says from behind me. I whip around, surprised to see her leaning against the doorframe.

"Why are you home early?" Theo asks, his brow furrowing as his gaze rakes over her. "And why do you look like you were crying?"

"Because I was," she says, offering us a weak smile.

"Because of me?" I ask, her words registering in my stubborn brain. It seems the guys were right. I've hurt her unknowingly, and I hate myself for it. Lo is my everything. I never want her to feel like she's not.

"Because of the situation," she quietly replies, pushing off the doorway. "I talked with Jazz." She holds up one hand when I open my mouth to speak. "And I'm not apologizing for that. I should have talked to her months ago, but I didn't want to disrespect your wishes."

"I don't want others knowing our business," I say, working hard to keep the anger from my voice. It's bad enough I can't knock her up. The last thing I need is everyone in our circle finding out.

"She's my best friend, Saint. She won't gossip." She steps closer, and I note the redness surrounding her sad eyes.

"Come here, baby." Theo opens his arms, and she readily falls into them. He squeezes his eyes shut as he holds her to him, pressing kisses into her hair.

A sob rips from her mouth, and it kills me. It fucking kills me. How did I not see this?

"Lo," I croak, taking a step toward her, but Theo shakes his head, cautioning me to stay back.

"I'm so sorry, Saint," she cries, her words muffled against Theo's chest. "I hate that I'm letting you down, but I can't keep doing this. It's destroying me."

Everything locks up inside me. "You don't want a baby with me?" I hear how cold my voice is, but her words are tearing strips off my heart.

"No!" She lifts her head, pinning me with tearstained sad eyes.

My breath stutters in my chest, and I rub at the piercing ache ripping across my ribcage.

"I mean yes," she quickly replies, shucking out of Theo's arms. "This isn't coming out right." She strides to me, cupping my face in her hands. "Of course, I want a baby with you. I love you, Saint. Nothing would make me happier."

"But?" 'Cause I sense one coming.

She lowers her hands to her sides. "But it's not going to happen unless we make changes."

"I don't understand."

Her tongue darts out, wetting her lips, and she bites on the corner of her mouth. I have a sudden urge to kiss her, to kiss all her worries away, but I don't think she'd appreciate it right now. "Can we sit down?" She gestures toward the couch.

"Do you want us to go, Lo?" Theo asks.

She shakes her head. "No, please stay. We need to resolve this as a family." She looks around, and her brows knit together. "Where are the kids?"

"With Freya. They won't be home for a while," Galen says. "We had planned on talking with Saint," he tacks on the end when he sees the confusion on her face.

"You had?" she asks, her gaze jumping between us.

"We knew you were upset last night, and we've noticed things seem stressed between you two," Theo explains.

"We have tried to respect your privacy," Galen adds. "But we realize now we made a mistake. We shouldn't have let it get this far. You're both upset, and this impacts all of us."

"We've always done things together," Caz says. "And we'll get through this together."

I don't see how, not when I'm the one who needs, wants, *craves*, to put a baby in her belly, but I keep those thoughts to myself.

We all sit, and I reach out, taking Lo's hand in mine, lacing our fingers together. "Have I been hurting you?"

Her eyes well up again, and I hate myself in this moment. "Yes," she softly admits. "I know you don't mean to. I know you're just focused on getting me pregnant, but it's almost like I don't matter anymore. Like I'm just a baby-making machine, a vessel for you to impregnate, and I can't even get that right." Tears spill down her cheeks, and I can hardly talk over the messy ball clogging my throat.

"No, Lo. That's not who you are to me." I brush tears off her cheeks. "I want a baby so badly with you. I want a child who is a part of me and a part of you. I want to see if he or she looks more like you or me and whether he or she resembles Bishop or either of our girls. But I don't want that at the expense of our relationship, because no one or nothing means more to me than you. I'm sorry if my actions have made you doubt that. Doubt me." I peer into her eyes. "I love you so much. You're my queen."

She smiles softly as fresh tears flow from her eyes. "I want to see what our child would look like too. Trust me when I say I want to have our baby as badly as you do. But everything is messed up." Her chest heaves, and she pauses for a second. Her lower lip trembles. "When was the last time you kissed me, Saint? Or the last time you held me in your arms for no reason other than wanting to feel me close? When was the last time you spontaneously made love to me because you wanted to, not because we were on a schedule?"

I pin her with an incredulous look, because she's being ridiculous. I know I might have been a bit obsessive about fucking her when she was ovulating, but it's not like it's been a chore or that I've stopped being affectionate with her. "I kissed you last night when we were in bed," I tell her.

She shakes her head, sadness washing over her face. "No, you didn't, Saint. You stripped me and fucked me like I was some nameless, faceless vagina, telling me how perfect the timing was and this was going to be the month. Then you came, and when I didn't want you to touch me, you made me sit on pillows and wait for fifteen minutes so your sperm could reach my egg."

My mind revisits last night, and I replay it, scene for scene, dismayed to discover she's right. How have I been so blind? I go further back, trying to remember the last time I kissed her, and I can't recall it. I feel sick. She's right. The guys are right, and I just didn't see it. I won't defend myself by mentioning how depressed I've been month after month when her period arrived. Or how stressed I've been at the thought I might not be able to father children, because making excuses just won't cut it. There is no acceptable justification for shutting her out. For treating her so coldly. I'm disgusted with myself.

Have I been so obsessed that I've forgotten everything she means to me? All that is important?

Theo looks at me with genuine concern, Caz looks shellshocked, and Galen looks like he's two seconds away from slicing my head off my shoulders. I wouldn't blame any of them for ripping me a new one. I've been so single-minded, so focused on the goal, I've lost sight of what matters. I've lost sight of my wife, and I haven't treated her right. I haven't loved her and cherished her like I vowed to, and I'm full of self-hatred. I'm disgusted I was so wrapped up in my head, in what I wanted and needed, I failed to see how I was hurting her.

Shame smacks into me on all sides, and I hang my head. A tight pain rips across my chest, and intense pressure settles on my shoulders. I have let everyone down, and it's time to man up and accept responsibility. Lifting my chin, I stare at my beautiful, brave wife. "You're right, Lo. I'm sorry. So, so sorry."

Her arm slides around my back. "I just want my husband back," she says over a sob. "I just want you to love me and for things to go back to the way they were before."

That shakes me out of my melancholy. I have never stopped loving her. That's a virtual impossibility. "Baby." I hold her face in my hands. "You have always been my queen, and that hasn't changed. I might have lost my way, but I have never stopped loving you. You're my world. I'm so sorry for how I've been treating you. The last thing I ever want to do is hurt you." Tears prick my eyes. "I just want a baby with you." My eyes lower to her flat stomach. "I dream of seeing your belly swollen with my kid. Besides you, it's the only thing I've ever wanted this much."

"I know, honey." She presses her forehead to mine, and I drop my hands, taking hers. "And I want that too, but I don't think we're going to get pregnant if we continue with the regimented routine because it's stressing me out and making me unhappy."

"That stops now. I promise." Her relieved smile

loosens some of the knots in my shoulders. "What do you suggest?" I ask, peering into her gorgeous green eyes.

"Let's drop all the planning and just go back to the way we were. Fucking when we want, not when we have to. Let it happen naturally. We don't have to rush this."

"What if it doesn't happen?" I ask because we might as well get everything out on the table. I've been afraid to voice this fear, as if saying the words out loud might make it real. "What if there's something wrong … with me?"

She flings her arms around me, squeezing me tight. My arms band around her warm body, and a sense of contentment—the kind that's been missing these past few months— seeps deep into my bones. I hold her tight, closing my eyes, savoring the feel of her pressed against me. "I bet there is nothing wrong other than us trying to force it," she says after a while, easing back so she's looking at me. "But if it doesn't happen by next year, we can talk to a specialist."

"Okay." I nod.

Her eyes fill with tears again, and it's unlike Lo to be so emotional. Maybe she's … I stop my train of thought because I've got to let it go. Nothing is more important to me than my wife. Not even a baby, although it's everything my heart desires. But making things right with Lo takes precedence. I hate that I've hurt her. That I've left her feeling like I don't love her anymore. Rectifying that is all that's important now.

"Really?" Her eyes spark with hope.

"Yes." I kiss her cheek. "I want to make it up to you. I can't promise it will be smooth sailing, but—"

"I know who you are, Saintly." She cuts across me, smirking, and I can't remember the last time she took that teasing tone with me. "And I know who I am. I kinda lost my way too, but not anymore. I won't let you force the agenda."

"We won't either," Galen says. I'd almost forgotten they were there.

"You two should go away next weekend," Theo suggests. "Take Lo someplace special for your birthday."

"Would you like that?" I ask, brushing loose strands of hair off her face.

"I would love that." The dreamy expression on her face unravels the last of the tension in my body.

"Consider it done then." I run my thumb along her lower lip, and she visibly shivers. Her eyes flash with heat in a way I haven't seen for a while. I kiss the corner of her mouth. "I love you."

Her eyes turn glassy again as she smiles. "I love you too."

I open my mouth—to ask permission to kiss her—before I mentally slap myself upside the head. I'm Saint fucking Westbrook, and I need no permission to kiss my beautiful wife. Lowering my head, I claim her lips with mine, and every part of my body rejoices as her lush mouth moves against mine.

CHAPTER 6

Harlow

"WANT SOME COMPANY?" Caz says later that night, entering my bedroom. I set my book down and smile at my husband.

"I'd love some." It's amazing how much lighter I feel after the family talk earlier. Saint and I went for a walk on the beach while the others went to meet up with Freya. We talked and talked for hours, cuddled and kissed, and we both needed that. Being with him like that again reminded me of everything we've been missing out on, and I can't wait for our romantic getaway this weekend. Saint is insisting on organizing it and he wants to keep it a secret until Friday. I'm already on a countdown.

Peeling back the covers, I pat the empty space beside me. Caz shucks out of his sweatpants, climbing into the bed in only his boxers. He opens his arms, and I settle my head on his bare chest. "You're so warm." I nuzzle in closer, my fingers lightly tracing the ink on his chest. The guys got them done last year—a large heart with my name and the kids' names inside. They left space for the planned future addition to the family, and I truly hope they'll be updating their ink next year. I have all their names, along with the kids' names, inked on the inside of my right arm, and every time I look at them, it brings the biggest smile to my face. Caz's strong arms tighten around me, and I briefly close my eyes, savoring being held by him. "You always make me feel so protected." I sigh in contentment when Caz's hand weaves through my hair.

"I'm glad because I would go to the ends of the earth for you, queenie."

I press a kiss to his chest, right over his heart, where the family ink rests. "I know you would. As I would for you too." I look up at him, spotting the telltale purple shadows under his eyes and frowning. "What's keeping you awake at night?"

His eyes lower to mine, and I get lost in the warm brown depths. "You and Saint were part of it. I'm glad we talked things through."

"Me too, and it's going to be okay." He nods, and I can tell he's happy we are getting things back on track. "Is it your mom?"

"Yeah." His face showcases his concern.

"Has something happened?" Have I been too self-absorbed to notice his pain?

"Not really. It's just that Nelia says she's very down

and her mobility isn't great."

Caz's dad survived the shootout at Galen's house the night Sinner died, but he was subsequently arrested, charged, and imprisoned, along with several other surviving Sainthood members. He died three years ago in jail—from lung cancer—only a few months before he was scheduled to be released. Mrs. Evans divorced him a couple years after he was incarcerated, and it helped to rebuild the bond with all her children. Caz bought his mom a new house in a nicer part of Prestwick, and his younger siblings still live with her. Nelia turned twenty-two recently, and Jake is eighteen. He just graduated high school.

We discovered Caz's mom had Parkinson's just after we found out about Bishop's heart condition. It was a stressful time for Caz. I know being so far away plays on his mind, and I wonder if we are selfish to stay in Rhode Island. If we shouldn't consider uprooting our lives and returning to Prestwick or Lowell, even if the thought doesn't hold much appeal.

"Why don't you go visit her this week? I know Theo is busy with work, but I could take a couple days off to go with you?" I offer. "We could bring the kids. They'd love to see their grandma."

"I appreciate the suggestion, but it doesn't make sense. We'll be vacationing there next month," he reminds me.

Every August, we return to Lowell to spend time with Caz's family and to catch up with Bry. He has his own tattoo shop now, and business is booming. He's been with his girlfriend, Deana, for years, though neither of them seems in any hurry to get hitched. We spend a week at the house on Galen's family grounds—the kids adore playing in the maze—and then we travel to Arizona to spend a week with Mom and Lincoln. They are married now and happy running a successful law practice in their local town. Diesel and Denise try to coordinate it so they are there at the same time, and our kids love playing with their girls.

"And the garage is fully booked this week," Caz continues. "Plus, Harry is on vacation, and we can't afford to be another man down." As a business owner, you'd think you could take time off whenever you want, but the reality is often the opposite.

"That's a shame, but you're right. Maybe we should send your mom some flowers, or I could talk to Nelia about booking them both in for a spa day?" I look into his eyes. "Do you think she'd like that?"

He kisses the tip of my nose. "I think that might cheer her up, and it's very thoughtful." He squeezes me gently. "Thank you."

"Do you ever wish you lived closer? That we'd move?" I ask, swirling circles on his chest with the tip of my finger. "Because we can discuss it with the others, if you like?"

He tilts my chin up. "You'd do that for me?" His tone drips with incredulity. And I get it. He knows I'm not keen on returning to the area we grew up in, for a whole heap of reasons.

"Of course, I would if that's what you need to happen." And I mean it. They are not idle words.

He lowers his mouth to mine, kissing me tenderly. "I love the way you love me, Lo."

"The feeling is definitely mutual." I smile against his lips.

"And I appreciate the offer so much, but I wouldn't ask that of any of you. I don't want to uproot the kids. They are happy here, and I know it'd be painful for everyone to move back there. Especially you and Theo."

Theo's family situation hasn't changed, and though he says he doesn't care—that he's moved past his parents' abandonment of him—we all know it's an ongoing source of pain because of the impact it has had on his relationship with his siblings. Theo meets up with his sister Ria a few times a year. She's three years younger than him, and she's a doctor. She works in Jefferson City, Missouri, and she's engaged to a fellow doctor. Ria is super sweet, and I'm glad Theo has a good relationship with her. The twins are a different matter. They are seventeen now and starting senior year soon, but Theo has little contact with them.

They were very young when his parents kicked Theo out of the house, so they didn't have time to form a bond. They are virtual strangers, and despite Ria's constant attempts to coax them into meeting with Theo, their parents have poisoned their minds to their brother, and they make no effort to get to know him. That hurts Theo. More than he will ever admit. I can only hope, when the twins mature and get older, they will see things in a different light and reach out to him.

"Would your mom and your brother and sister ever

consider moving here?" I throw out the idea as it pops into my head. "We could find a nice place close by for her and help her sell her place in Prestwick? The Newport sea air might do wonders for her mood."

Caz blinks a couple of times. "Why didn't I think of that?" His eyes light up. "Nelia only has one more year left in college, and Jake wants an apprenticeship after he graduates high school. He could come work with me or Saint in either of the garages." I can almost see his brain contemplating the pros and cons. He plants a firm kiss on my lips. "You're a fucking genius, Lo. This is the perfect solution. I honestly don't think my family is that invested in Prestwick. It holds a lot of bad memories for them too." He glances at his watch, whipping the covers off. "It's not too late to call them." Grabbing his sweats off the floor, he hurriedly pulls them on. He crawls over the bed, kissing me again. "I love you."

"Love you too." I hold on to his face, demanding more kisses.

He chuckles as his lips brush against mine. "Don't worry, queenie. I'll be back, and you're definitely due a reward."

Desire coils low in my belly. "Damn straight I am." I swat his butt as he climbs off the bed. "Don't take too long. I'll just be here naked, touching myself while I imagine it's your hands covering my body."

He slams to a halt, peering at me over his shoulder. "Fucking hell, Lo. I'm hard as a rock now."

Giggling, I yank my nightdress up over my head, tossing it away. I cup my breasts, toying with my nipples, as I lick my lips, pouting seductively in his direction. "Chop, chop, Caz. Go make your momma happy, and then come back and make your wife happy."

CHAPTER 7

Harlow

"THIS PLACE IS gorgeous," I say, as Saint comes up behind me, circling his arms around my waist. I lean back into his hard chest, admiring the stunning coastline in front of me. The small golden sandy beach is private, accessible only by residents, so it truly is the perfect get-away spot.

"I'm glad you approve," he purrs, pushing my new lavender-striped hair aside so he can plant kisses along one side of my neck. "I know we haven't gone far from home, but I didn't want to waste hours in the car."

I spin around in his embrace, looping my arms around his neck. "It's perfect, Saint. We have our own luxury cottage for the weekend, on this beautiful beach, and there is an abundance of restaurants, shops, and bars within walking distance. You couldn't have chosen better." I stretch up, kissing the corner of his mouth. "This weekend isn't about where we are, but the fact we are together. No distractions. No kids. Just us."

"Have I told you how much I love your new hair?" he says, threading his fingers through the long silky wavy strands cascading over my shoulders.

I grin. "You might have mentioned it a time or two." I wanted to go full lavender, but the hairdresser said that will take a few trips to accomplish, so we started with some lavender highlights today which she will gradually build upon until my hair is completely transformed. After years of wearing it dark, I'm excited for the change.

"You are stunning," he adds, and my heart melts. "With every passing year, you get even more beautiful."

"Or it could be your eyesight is getting worse," I quip, running my hands through his dark blond hair. Saint wore his hair cropped for years, but he's let it grow out now, and I love the mess of waves tumbling onto his brow. More for me to grab when we're in the throes of passion.

"There is nothing wrong with my eyesight, queenie." He flattens his palms over my ass, squeezing. "You're fucking gorgeous, and we're lucky bastards."

We move as one, our lips colliding in a passionate kiss I feel all the way to the tips of my toes. Saint has made a huge effort this week to prove his words from last weekend weren't thrown out in the moment. Every day, he's sent me flowers. My office at work resembles a florist. Then he booked Jazz and me in for a mani and pedi this morning along with a trip to the hair salon where I decided on a whim to dye my hair.

My other husbands haven't seen it yet since Saint picked me up from the hair salon and we drove straight here.

"I won't disagree with you," I tease, grinding my hips against his as he continues kneading the cheeks of my ass. "I *am* a fucking catch."

"And still so humble," he quips, thrusting his hips against mine.

Desire powers through me, and I slam my lips against his, devouring his mouth. I have missed kissing Saint. Missed feeling his tongue tangling with mine. Missed feeling the intensity of his love. He has made it a point to kiss and hug me every day, showering me with affection, and it's amazing how quickly things are returning to normal. Thank God, because I have missed my possessive alpha male like crazy.

Saint breaks our kiss, rubbing his thumb along my lips. "This mouth." His eyes darken with liquid lust. "I fucking love this mouth." He pecks my lips quickly. "And I have plans for it later." He winks, and my body floods with desire. "But right now, you need to get dressed, or we'll miss our dinner reservation."

Taking me by the hand, he leads me inside. The cottage isn't huge, but it's big enough with a large open-plan living space facing French door that opens out onto the wraparound deck. At the back of the property, there are two bedrooms, both with king-sized beds and en suite bathrooms. Saint leads me into the main bedroom, and my eyes pop wide at what is waiting for me on the bed. "You are really spoiling me," I say, striding toward the pretty dress laid out for me. "Anyone would think it's *my* birthday." I toss a quick smile over my shoulder, suffused with love for him. My fingers skim over the soft material of the dress, admiring the beautiful pink, purple, and silver floral print overlaid on top of the pristine white silk. I hold it up against me, glancing at my reflection in the mirror. "It goes perfectly with my hair," I muse. Happiness bubbles underneath the surface of my skin, and my heart soars.

"Do you really like it?" Saint asks. "I roped Jazz into helping me, but I wasn't quite sure if it was your style."

I know what he means. I don't usually wear something so vibrant, but it's absolutely gorgeous and it's Dior, so what's not to like?

Saint leaves me to get dressed, and I feel like a million dollars when I step out onto the deck an hour later, wearing my new dress and silver stilettos. "What do you think?" I ask, twirling, the silky material swishing around my hips and my calves with the motion. The dress is a halter style at the top with an empire waistline, and the skirted part flows down my body, ending with a hem of differing lengths. It feels gorgeous against my skin, and it's summery and elegant without being too over the top.

"Fuck me." Saint's gaze lingers as he roams the length of my body. "Why did I think it was a good idea to go out to eat?" he murmurs, stalking toward me with intent.

He looks hot in his black short-sleeved button-up shirt and ripped jeans, with a stylish layer of stubble on his chin and cheeks, and his untamed hair tumbling in sexy waves over his brow. His gorgeous blue eyes scream possession as he sweeps me into his arms. "I love this dress, but I really want to rip it off and worship every inch of your bare skin."

I plant my hands on his shoulders, inhaling the spicy, musky scent of his cologne. I fucking love how good he smells but not enough to say to hell with our plans. I don't want this weekend to be all about sex. Not when that's all our relationship has been about these past few months. I want to enjoy time with him outside the bedroom. To laugh and have fun and just enjoy being with my husband. "You can take a rain check because I'm all dolled up now and raring to go."

"I'll be calling in that rain check later." His eyes blaze with heat as he releases me, pulling his cell phone out of his pocket.

"I'm banking on it." I deliberately lick my lips and thrust out my chest, planting one hand on my hip and striking a pose.

"I need to take a photo for the guys. They will kill me otherwise."

I offer up my most seductive pout, angling my body in a few different poses while Saint snaps away.

"You're so fucking sexy," Saint says, swiping his fingers across the keypad. "The guys will go crazy when they see these." He shoots me a smug grin, repocketing his phone and offering me his arm.

I'm sensing ulterior motives, and it's classic Saint. "You just can't help yourself, can you?" I ask, looping my arm through his.

"Nope." He chuckles. "I still love rubbing their noses

in it."

Called it! "You're so competitive." I nestle into his side as he leads us down the steps and around the side of the house. "But I wouldn't have you any other way."

A half hour later, we are in a fashionable bar and grill, seated beside one another in a velvet-backed booth, as sultry beats reverberate in the background. "This place is awesome," I admit, taking another sip of my champagne cocktail.

"I thought you'd like it better than the Michelin-starred restaurant I almost booked."

I'm sure the food is exquisite if it's a Michelin-starred restaurant, but this place is more my vibe. "You did good, Saintly." I plant a lingering kiss on his cheek. "You did *real* good, and you're so getting laid later."

A warm hand lands on my thigh as he leans in, pressing his mouth to my ear. "I hope you weren't planning on getting much sleep because I want to reacquaint myself with every inch of your body."

I cup his face in my hands. "That is music to my ears, Saintly."

"Speaking of music..." Saint gently removes my hands from his face, entwining his fingers through mine. "Dance with me?" He arches a brow.

"I would love to." It doesn't matter that there is no one on the small dance floor at the rear of the bar or that everyone looks at us as Saint leads me to it because, for me, no one else exists but the man staring at me like I'm his everything. Saint twirls me around, dips me down low, and cradles me close as he unashamedly grinds his hips against mine, and we laugh and kiss as we dance, oblivious to our surroundings, only stopping when the waitress informs us our food is at our table.

We sit pressed against one another in the booth, feeding one another in between kisses, and I fall in love with him all over again.

We walk home along the beach, barefoot, wrapped around one another, and my heart is full, my mind light, the future bright.

"I love you, my queen," Saint says, holding his naked body still over me, peering deep into my eyes. I'm a writhing mass of desire underneath him, brought over the edge three times already as he remained true to his word, worshiping every part of my body like it was our first time together. Lust flows through my body like water gliding through a stream, and I'm more than ready to feel him moving inside me. "I will never make you forget that again."

"What's happened is in the past," I say, reaching up to brush my fingers along the stubble on his cheeks. "We just focus on moving forward now." There is nothing to be gained from overanalyzing the mistakes of the recent past.

He nods, and I feel him nudging my entrance. "I never want to treat you any less than you deserve. You have given me a life I never imagined possible, Lo, and you are my entire universe. You and the kids and our family mean everything to me." He pushes slowly inside me, and we both moan in pleasure. "This, babe." He thrusts to the hilt, holding himself still, fully seated inside me.

"This is everything."

Leaning down, he captures my mouth in a passionate kiss as he starts to move inside me. Except it's no frenetic coupling like the past few months. His thrusts are measured and slow, and he pulls out and pushes back in as if he has all the time in the world. I feel him moving inside me, and it's as magical as I remember. My walls hug his cock, clinging to him, and my fingers explore his warm skin, remembering all the contours and planes of his beautiful body.

He holds my wrists up over my head as his lips worship my lips and then my neck. His mouth moves lower, brushing seductively against my collarbone, sending shivers cascading along my flushed skin. Very softly, he sucks one nipple into his mouth while his hips continue moving strategically, his erection sliding in and out of me like time is endless. It's a slow, continual seduction, a synchronized marriage of tongue, lips, fingers, and cock as he blows my mind, entrances my body, and reclaims my heart.

I am putty in his hands, matching his languid thrusts, meeting his skillful explorations with explorations of my own, making love to his mouth in return, until there is no me and no him. We are one as we ascend into ecstasy, shattering explosively together, staring at one another through glassy eyes as all the cracks are repaired and we are remade anew.

CHAPTER 8

Harlow

WE MADE LOVE for hours, and Saint worshiped me like I was made of porcelain. It was an entirely new experience for us and one which we both craved like addicts in need of a new high. Eventually, we fell asleep, waking up in a tangle of limbs as a loud noise jolts us both from slumber.

"What the hell is that?" I mumble into his chest, struggling to open my eyes. My body aches deliciously in a way it hasn't for a long time, and I stretch out alongside him, purring like a cat in heat.

"Surprise, queenie," Saint mumbles as Galen, Caz, and Theo come bursting into the room.

"What are you guys doing here?" I ask, rubbing sleep from my eyes as Saint repositions us against the headboard.

"Gatecrashing the party," Caz says, flopping down on the end of the bed. "What else?" He flashes me a naughty grin.

"Who's watching the kids?" We don't have many babysitting options considering we live so far from our families.

"Jazz and Ken have them."

"Was this your doing?" I ask Saint, brushing my messy hair out of my eyes.

"Yep. It's been forever since we were all together. It didn't seem right to hog you for the whole weekend."

"This seriously feels like *my* birthday," I say, before remembering what day it is. I squeal, flinging my arms around Saint. "Happy birthday, baby." I pepper his handsome face with kisses while he looks at me with amusement.

"Yeah, happy birthday, baby," Caz says, putting his face into Saint's and puckering his lips.

Saint pushes him away, and he falls back, chuckling. "Knock that shit off, assface. Go kiss Theo."

"Been there, done that, bought the T-shirt," Theo says, smirking as he flips Saint off. Sitting down beside me, on the edge of the bed, he pecks my lips. "Love the hair." He fingers a few strands of my hair. "It's sexy as fuck."

"If we hadn't already arranged this," Galen says, crawling up the middle of the bed. "We'd have called in every favor to get our butts here after Saint sent us those photos last night." He leans in, kissing me. "I didn't think you could get any sexier, but fuck me, that hair is sensational."

"You all know sex is guaranteed, right?" I say, quirking a brow as my gaze dances between them. "You don't need to shower me with compliments. My pussy is yours. My mouth and my ass too." I fix the fakest sweet smile on my mouth as my hungry gaze rakes over them. It's been forever since we had group sex.

"I smell an orgy coming on." Caz waggles his brows and rubs his hands in glee.

"Food first," Galen says as his stomach grumbles loudly.

"You are getting old, dude," Saint says. "When does food ever come before sex?"

"When I need sustenance to show my wife the best fucking time." Galen tilts his head to the side, grinning. "And I'm officially the baby, so you don't get to throw shade."

"You're only a few months younger than us," Theo reminds him.

"I'm still only thirty. The rest of you are *ancient*."

"Hey!" I swat Galen with a pillow. "Anyone would think you don't want me to ride your cock."

He tosses the pillow aside, yanking me out of Saint's arms and plonking me on his lap. "Does a bear shit in the woods? The day I stop wanting you to ride my *monster* cock is the day I'm dead."

"You just had to go there, didn't you?" Saint shakes his head before swinging his legs out of the side of the bed. He yawns, and that sets me off too.

"Can't deny the facts," Galen teases, puffing out his chest.

"I still can't believe y'all measured your dicks," I say. "I seriously have no words." There is competitive, and then there are my husbands. "Where are you going?" I ask, when Saint stands.

"To take a piss." He pins me with a cocky smile. "Unless you want to hold it?"

"Ew. There are some things even *I* won't do. Be gone with you." I shoo him away with my hands, and the instant he steps into the en suite bathroom, I hop up, racing naked for my weekend bag. Bending over, I rummage around until I find the envelope.

Warm hands land on my hips, and I shriek at the unexpected contact. "Hell yeah, beautiful," Caz says, rocking his hips suggestively as he thrusts back and forth against my ass. "Just like that, queenie."

Straightening up, I fist the envelope and my silk robe in one hand, playfully shoving my husband away. "Someone's horny."

"We're all horny," Galen adds. "Just in case there's any confusion."

"I don't know why we bothered bringing overnight bags," Theo says. "Not when we'll be naked for most of the time."

"You guys have this all worked out, hmm?" I tease, laughing at Caz's pout when I wrap my knee-length red silk robe around my body, tying the belt.

"Yes," Caz replies. "And wearing robes was *not* part of the plan." He tugs on the belt, and my robe falls open. "That's much better," he murmurs, his eyes darkening with lust. Reaching underneath my robe, he cups one of my breasts. "Much, much better."

I swat his hand away. "There will be plenty of time for sex. I want to give Saint his birthday gift, have breakfast, and then the orgy can commence in earnest." I flash him a devilish grin as I firmly tie my robe again.

"What gift?" Saint asks, yawning again as he emerges from the bathroom, buck ass naked. His dick juts out proudly, saluting me, and I lick my lips as desire tightens in my core.

Theo chuckles, and Galen grins. Saint bundles me into his arms. "Is that for me?" He gestures at the envelope in my hand.

I turn around in his embrace, smiling. "Yes." I give it to him, my grin expanding as he lets me go to tear at the paper.

"No. Way." Awe seeps from his tone, and his eyes pop wide as he stares at the photograph while palming the car keys in his hand. "Is this real?" He lifts his head, eyeballing me and then the guys. "You seriously found me a 1969 Ford Mustang Boss 429?" Shock splays across his face.

Since I relocated my dad's car collection from the cabin to Newport ten years ago, Saint has become obsessed with classic cars. We don't get to visit the cabin much these days, so it seemed a shame to let the cars gather dust. The guys were in complete agreement, and we built a new garage at our house to accommodate them. Now, we have more cars than we know what to do with, but that still hasn't stopped the guys from adding to the collection.

While Saint runs the business side of the garages he co-owns with Caz, and Caz is the more hands-on of the pair, he still loves tinkering with cars as a hobby. Saint got it into his head that he wanted a 1969 Ford Mustang Boss and he's spent years scouring the internet to find one he could fix up, with no success.

"I located a guy online who specializes in finding classic cars," I explain. "I actually contacted him almost two years ago, hoping to find one for your thirtieth birthday, but it didn't work out. He got in touch last month to let me know one was going under auction and he bid on it for us."

When Saint discovers we paid over two hundred thousand for it, he'll lose his nut, but he'll get years and years of enjoyment out of it, and he'll have something special to pass down to one of the kids when they are older. Besides, it's actually a good investment. They are so rare I doubt we'd have trouble recouping our money if he chose to sell it in years to come.

"It's got the A code engine, and it's in pretty decent shape," Caz says. "But the bodywork and interiors need work. I figured we could work on it together in the evenings. It will be at the Newport garage on Monday."

Saint stares between the picture of his car and us, his head jerking up and down, and for once, he's completely lost for words.

Caz chuckles. "He's speechless."

"We need to record this moment," Theo adds.

"At least we now know how to shut him up," Galen says.

"Assholes," Saint mutters, flipping his middle finger up as his gaze stays locked on the picture of his car.

I had planned on cooking Saint breakfast in bed. Okay, well I was going to attempt it, but now the guys are here, they won't let me near the kitchen. I consider that a win. Saint does too. So, we sit outside on the lounge chairs while the others slave over a hot stove. We are wearing our swimwear, sipping mimosas, as we listen to the waves lap against the shore. The day is bright and clear, and there isn't a cloud in the sky. Heat beats down on us, and I tilt my face up to the sun, absorbing the warmth from its rays.

"Is it okay that I arranged for them to come?" he asks, touching my arm.

I angle my head to face him. "It's perfect. I'm glad you did."

"We're a team," he adds, idly rubbing my arm. Closing my eyes, I savor his touch and the deep sense of contentment I feel. "I didn't just need to make it right with you. I needed to make it right with my brothers too."

"I know, hun." I lean over and kiss him. "I'm happy we are all together again. In fact, I think it's time we made it a rule. We should have at least one weekend a year where we sneak away."

If we prearrange it, I can get Mom and Linc to fly in to watch the kids. She loves any opportunity to spend time with her grandchildren. Or, if Caz's family moves to Rhode Island, I'm sure Nelia would babysit with Grandma Evans.

Howie could be an option, if he wasn't the eternal

bachelor. I would feel nervous leaving him alone with the rugrats for a weekend, because he's clueless when it comes to kids. Howie works with VERO now too, in a different section than Theo, but they work on some projects together, on occasion. Over the years, Saint found it in his heart to forgive his other uncle, and he's now a proper part of the family. He lives in D.C. and usually comes up for a weekend every two months or so.

After a delicious breakfast, we relax on the beach before taking a swim, and then we head back to the house, making a beeline for the bedroom.

"Oh God. Yes, Galen. Just like that. That feels so fucking good," I moan, as he tilts his hips up, his cock hitting the perfect spot inside me while I bounce up and down on top of him.

"It's no wonder he has a big head," Saint says, reaching around to cup my tits. He kneads them roughly as he thrusts in and out of my ass. "You give him far too much credit."

"Jealous 'cause I've got a monster cock and I know how to use it?" Galen quips in between primal moans.

"As if," Saint scoffs. "Tell them how good I made you feel last night, baby." He nips at my earlobe before planting hot kisses along the side of my neck.

"You sexed me good, Saintly. You *loved* me good." I stretch my head around, and his lips glide against mine without hesitation.

"If you're done with the pissing contest, some of us are feeling left out," Caz says, and I can hear the pout in his tone.

I tear my lips from Saint's, whimpering as he and his cousin lay siege to my body in a crescendo of expert moves and scorching-hot touches. Fuck, I have missed this.

"Don't pretend like you and Theo haven't been having your own little party," I tease, reaching out to cup Caz's face. "I saw you sucking one another off."

"Fuck. Angel," Galen hisses, as liquid warmth gushes from my pussy. Watching Caz and Theo together will never get old. It turns me on like you wouldn't believe.

"Well, we need your mouth now, babe," Theo confirms, sliding up on the other side of the bed.

I lean into him, planting a passionate kiss on his mouth. "Hmm. I can taste Caz's cock on your lips."

Caz's fingers replace Saint's on one breast, and he tweaks my nipple between his thumb and his forefinger. "My turn, queenie. I need that dirty mouth."

Angling around, I kiss Caz, sliding my tongue between his lush lips, letting him taste himself. His mouth is quickly replaced with his cock, and I alternate between the lovers, taking turns sucking them both, bringing them to the brink.

I come with Saint and Galen, and then we switch out. The cousins take seats by the window, smoking a joint as they watch us reposition ourselves. I lie beside Theo, running my hands up and down his lean body as Caz slides inside his ass. I watch, transfixed as he fucks my husband, and my hips grind against Theo's side of their own accord. "You two are so freaking hot together. I fucking love it." Theo grabs the nape of my neck, pulling my mouth to his as my fingers curl around his length. I stroke his hard length while Caz fucks his ass, and then I situate myself on top of Theo, and he holds my hips as I maneuver his dick into my pussy.

Heat rolls off Caz as he presses against my back, fucking Theo's ass while I ride Theo's cock. Sounds of skin slapping echo around the room along with mutual pants and groans. God, I love sex. I would spend twenty-four-seven naked, on my back, fucking my guys over and over, if I could get away with it.

"Thank fuck for yoga," I pant, as my leg and thigh muscles strain with the effort involved in fucking Theo like this.

"Let's move," Theo says, always thinking about my comfort.

I lie flat on my back while Theo hovers over me, slowly working his condom-covered dick inside me. Leaning down, he kisses me while jutting his butt up so Caz can glide into his puckered hole. We fuck with practiced ease, like lovers who have done this time and time again, while the two cousins get stoned in their chairs, watching us get our rocks off.

We spend the rest of the afternoon in the bedroom, only moving into the living area when hunger gets the better of all of us. After showering, we lie draped around one another on the couches, sipping drinks while we wait for our takeout to arrive. Galen is flicking channels on the TV, trying to find something worth watching.

"Wait!" Theo exclaims, bolting upright. "Go back to that sports channel."

"It's the Chicago Bears," Caz confirms, leaning his elbows on his knees.

"And there's their star quarterback," Saint adds.

I smile at the screen when Sean's handsome face appears. We have followed his career over the years, and we try to catch most of his games on TV. Sariah would be so proud of him. While he and Emmett both played ball in college, Sean is the only one who went on to the NFL. He was a third-round draft pick for the Bears, and he's lived in Chicago ever since. He got married last year to Lainey. She's a widow with three small kids. Her first husband was in the military and he lost his life in Afghanistan when she was pregnant with their youngest child.

Sean didn't date for years, throwing himself into his college studies and football, and I worried about him a lot, so I was thrilled when he met Lainey and even more thrilled a year later when he told me they were getting married. She's very different from Sariah, not that it's a bad thing. She's a few years older than us, and she runs her own psychiatrist practice. I have enormous respect for her. I can't even imagine how hard it must have been to raise kids alone while studying and working. I'm not terribly close to her, but we get along fine when we do meet. Which isn't often, but I make it a point to keep in contact with Sean by phone, and we speak a few times a year. He's my last link to Sariah, and I never want to lose touch.

I lost touch with Emmett years ago, and I know Sean rarely hears from him anymore. It's hard to keep in contact with everyone when we are all spread out and everyone leads busy lives. All I know is Emmett is happy living in Texas with his wife and two kids and he has a successful electrical engineering career.

We watch the game, rooting for our friend, while we dig into our Thai food and enjoy a few beers. When the doorbell chimes a short while later, I get up, taking the box with the cake into the kitchen. Theo helps me light the candles, and we all sing happy birthday to Saint. "Make a wish, Saintly," I say, holding the cake out in front of him.

"I already have, queenie." He holds my gaze as he blows out the candles in one go. No one needs to ask him what he wished for because we already know.

THE SAINTHOOD

EPILOGUE

Harlow

Six months later

MY HANDS SHAKE as I park the car at the curb, killing the engine before taking a moment to compose myself. My heart is beating frantically behind my rib cage, and hope bubbles underneath the surface of my skin. I pray I haven't made a mistake coming here, because I never want to hurt Saint, but I have a good feeling about it, and I don't want to do this without him.

Forcing my nerves aside, I climb out of my SUV, locking it with the key fob as I walk toward the entrance to the garage.

"What's wrong?" Saint asks the second he sees me. "Did Bishop get into trouble at school again?"

I shake my head as I stride toward the reception desk.

"Not that I'm aware of, and I'm sure Galen would've called me if there was an issue."

Bishop started elementary school last year, and it's been eventful, to say the least. He has a higher than normal level of intelligence for his age, and he isn't fitting in easily. He has one best friend, Hayes, but he regularly gets into arguments with a couple of the other boys in his class, and it has caused some friction. We've been called in a few times to meet with his teacher and the principal, and we're not convinced the private school we enrolled him in is the right fit.

Bishop takes it all in stride, and it doesn't seem to upset him, but we can't help worrying. We have considered moving him, but he doesn't want to go to a new school because he is best buds with Hayes and he doesn't want to be separated from him. Also, Luna will be joining him in August, and he wants to go to the same school as his sister so he can look out for her. His words, not mine.

"Is it Rora?" Saint asks, stepping out from behind the desk to greet me. He kisses me softly before bundling me up in his arms.

"Nope. She's home with Galen this week. Remember?" Rora started preschool in September, and there have been some issues there too although she seems to have settled down recently. They are on a break this week, and Galen is enjoying having her and Luna around more than usual.

"Okay. I'm obviously way off track," he murmurs into my hair.

"Can't a wife just drop by her husband's garage

without there being a reason?" I ask even though there *is* a reason I'm here, but I really should drop by more often. We could do lunch after my shift at the center some days.

"Of course, you can. I'm just surprised to see you, but it's not unwelcome. I haven't eaten yet," he adds, winding his fingers through my lavender hair. "Let me take you out for lunch."

"That sounds wonderful. But we need to do something first."

He arches a brow, and I swallow over the anxious lump in my throat as I thrust the small paper bag into his hand. He opens it, sucking in a gasp as he removes the pregnancy test.

"There is a reason," he whispers, sounding like he's in a daze. When he lifts his head, there are tears in his eyes. "Do you really think you—"

"I'm two weeks late, Saint," I admit, cutting across him. I didn't want to say anything earlier, because we don't do this anymore. Since we had our heart to heart, we have relaxed on all fronts. Where Saint used to force me to pee on a stick every month, now he just waits for me to mention my period. The fact it's been this long and he didn't even ask about it shows how far we have come. I'm not naive to think he doesn't remember, but he doesn't force the issue. Things are great between us again, but there is always this little niggle at the back of everything, and we all feel it.

"I'm scared," he says, his voice sounding choked. "And excited," he adds, his eyes lighting up.

"Me too, but this feels different." That's as close as I will come to saying it.

A look of steely determination washes over his face as he shoves the bag into my purse and takes my hand. "Let's do this." He leads me into the garage, and the guys wave and call out as we pass.

My chest heaves when I enter Saint's private bathroom at the side of his office. Saint locks the door while I wipe my clammy hands down the front of my yoga pants, reminding myself to breathe.

"My queen." Saint clasps my face in his hands. "Don't be nervous. Whatever it says, we will deal with it together." He rests his forehead against mine. "If it's meant to be, it will happen."

I press a hard kiss to his lips. "I fucking love you, Saint Westbrook."

"Love you too, babe," he says as I get down to business.

We hold one another after I'm done while we wait for the stick to show the result. It's the longest three minutes of my life.

"Lo," Saint whispers, glancing over my shoulder.

Keeping a hold of his hand, I ease out of his arms and pluck the digital stick up, reading the words through blurry eyes.

"You're pregnant," he rasps, taking the stick from me with trembling hands. He stares at it while happy tears roll down my face. "You're having my baby." Tears stream shamelessly down his cheeks as he sets the test down, gently placing his hands on my stomach. "We did it. My baby is growing in there."

I fling my arms around him, half laughing and half crying, and he lifts me up, carefully swinging me around, dotting kisses all over my face. Setting my feet down on the ground, he pins me with a wide smile, pressing a loving kiss to my mouth. "I love you, Harlow. I love you so fucking much. You've just made all my dreams come true."

SAINT

Seven months later

"CONGRATULATIONS," THE MIDWIFE says. "You have a son." She hands our baby to me, and I cradle him to my chest, barely able to see him through the tears flowing down my face. My chest heaves with indecipherable emotion as I look at my flesh and blood for the first time. He has a fine layer of downy dark hair on his head, and his features are all scrunched up, his eyes closed, lashes fluttering, as he adjusts to life outside the womb.

He's tiny. Barely weighing anything in my arms, and my protective instincts kick in, like they did with our other kids. I would kill for this child. I would annihilate anyone who sought to hurt him. I press a kiss to his temple, uncaring he's still covered in bits of blood and fluids. The nurse gave him a cursory quick cleaning before wrapping him in a soft towel and handing him to me because she could tell I couldn't wait a minute more before cradling my son in my arms.

The surge of emotion flooding my system is unlike anything I've felt before. "Welcome to the world, little man," I whisper. "I've waited a long time to meet you."

It's hasn't actually been that long even though it took over a year for Lo to get pregnant. That's not long compared to how long other couples have to wait. But I'm an impatient prick, and those fourteen months felt like fourteen years.

We made the most of our time though, and we remodeled the nursery to accommodate the twins, fitting it out with everything they need. We even picked their names after the scan confirmed we were expecting a boy and a girl. We knew the chances of Lo giving birth early were high, so we wanted to be well prepared. Twins are usually born around thirty-five weeks, and with Lo having given birth to three kids previously, it was a pretty foregone conclusion we'd be welcoming the newest additions to our family at this time.

Holding my son, Soren, in my arms, is the best fucking feeling in the world. All I need now is my daughter Willow to be born, and for my wife to be okay, and everything will be perfect.

This isn't the first time I've been in the delivery room with my wife. Galen and I were with her when Bishop was born, and Theo and I were with Lo when Luna was born. Caz and Theo supported her at Rora's birth. It's ironic, or kismet, that all of us ended up being there when our biological kids were born. We asked the others if one of them wanted to be with us today, but they declined, stating they wanted to be with the other kids, to help keep them entertained in case the labor was long.

I'm not sure if that's the truth. Maybe they were letting us have this moment together because it's the first time Lo has given birth knowing who the biological father is. Or maybe they are pandering to the possessive side of my personality. I'm not even sure if the medical team would've permitted anyone else in, as there is a higher risk when delivering more than one baby. Whatever the reason, I'm glad it's just Lo and me. Fuck it if that makes me selfish. It makes it more special, especially after everything we've been through to get to this point.

Lo grunts, gripping the side of the bed, and I crouch down, bringing our son close to her, figuring she needs the incentive to deliver his sibling. I have never been more in awe of my wife than I am today. She's so strong. So beautiful. A warrior. A queen. The love of my fucking life. The mother of my children. The owner of my heart and soul.

Lo is a fucking trooper, and I don't know how she has the strength to keep going, but she doesn't complain much. She is just getting on with it. I will never feel worthy of this woman.

"Say hi to Mommy," I tell Soren, and a loud wail rips from his lips. I slide my finger in his hand, silently fist pumping the air when his tiny fingers curl around mine. Fresh tears prick my eyes, and I'm barely holding it together.

Lo breathes in and out, gritting her teeth as she looks at our baby boy. "Is he okay?" she asks in between pants.

"He's perfect," I say just as the nurse arrives to take him away to be bathed. "He's got a fine set of lungs anyway." Wringing the cloth in the bowl of water by the bed, I dab at Lo's brow, wiping beads of sweat away and brushing sticky strands of hair off her face.

"Just another few seconds and then one big push, sweetie," the midwife says from between her legs.

I slide my arm around Lo's back and hold her hand, inhaling and exhaling with her as she prepares to bear down.

"Now, Harlow," the midwife commands, and Lo grits her teeth, panting and groaning as she delivers our daughter.

Piercing cries ring out as our daughter comes kicking and screaming into the world.

Lo slumps against me, and I press a fierce kiss to her temple while the nurse cleans our little girl and the midwife attends to my wife. "I love you," I tell her. "I love you so much. You have made me the happiest man alive today." I don't hide my tears as I kiss and hold her.

"I love you too," she says, crying happy tears and smiling as the nurse hands our daughter over. "Wow. She's going to be blonde." She smooths a finger gently over the blonde hair stuck to our daughter's head.

"I wonder if she'll have curls like Luna," I muse, sniffing as powerful emotion sneaks up on me again.

The nurse returns our son, all clean and smelling like

lavender baby bath, wrapped in a long-sleeved onesie under the soft blue blanket we brought with us. We coo over him while we wait for our daughter to be bathed and returned, and then I go out to get the others.

Our family bursts into the room, and the noise levels elevate a few decibels as Rora squeals in excitement. Caz has to wrangle her into his arms to stop her from lunging at her new brother and sister. Luna snuggles with Lo, smiling as she holds her new sister in both their arms, while I cradle my son in my arms, showing him off to Bishop.

"See that," I tell our eldest son, speaking loudly so the whole room hears. "That's evidence of super, super, super sperm." I knocked our woman up with two kids. Two babies, motherfuckers. None of those assholes managed that.

"Saintly!" Lo shrieks.

I smirk, slanting a smug look in Galen, Caz, and Theo's direction. "Admit it, motherfuckers," I add, uncaring about cussing. There is no way to protect our kids from cussing in our household. "I'm the fucking bomb." I puff out my chest, my heart swelling with joy.

"We're never going to hear the end of this," Galen mutters, but he's grinning. He slaps me on the shoulder. "I'm happy for you, man."

"He looks just like Lo," Caz says, leaning in to coo at our new son. "Thank fuck."

"Our new daughter is the spitting image of her daddy," Lo adds, gazing adoringly at the tiny little princess in her arms. "So, suck it up, Caz," she teases.

"Yeah, Poppa Bear," Rora says, jutting out her lower lip. "Suck it up!"

Laughter surrounds us, and as I cast my gaze over my family, I offer up thanks to whoever graced us with these two new miracles, promising I will never let them or any of our kids down.

Turn the page to read a special Valentine's bonus scene! I originally wrote this based on a poll in my reader's group on Facebook. I'm including it here in case you haven't had the chance to read it! Enjoy.

VALENTINE'S BONUS SCENE

Theo

"POPPA BEAR," RORA semi-whispers, tugging on Caz's leg as we hover outside the master bedroom. "Why do we have to wait out here?" Her lower lip juts out, and she pins her bio dad with doe eyes that usually get her everything she wants.

"Because they want to sex on Mom first, stupid," Bishop replies before Caz can get a word in.

My eyes pop wide, Caz chuckles, and Saint fights a grin.

I think we'll be having a little man-to-man chat with Bishop later. I bet that little shit Hayes said something to him. Bishop's best friend has four older brothers, and the stuff that comes out of his mouth is completely inappropriate at times. Bishop is only seven, and I want him to remain a child for as long as possible. Kids grow up too fucking fast, and I don't want that for any of our children.

"Prodigy." Galen slants a stern look in our eldest son's direction. "Watch your language, and what have I told you about calling your sister that?"

"She's annoying," Bishop says, crossing his arms. "Why does everything have to be about her?"

"Entertaining as this is," Saint says, "we need to move this along. Soren is stirring," he adds, rocking his sleepy son in his arms. We got up earlier when the twins woke for a feed and were careful not to wake Lo. She's still breastfeeding, and we wanted to give her the opportunity to sleep in late for a change. Saint forced her into expressing last night, so we had bottles on hand to feed the hungry monsters this morning.

"I think Willow would sleep through an earthquake," I say, cradling her close to my chest as I lean down to press a feather-soft kiss to her warm brow. The twins couldn't be more different in both looks and temperament. Soren is like a mini- Saint in the making. He's loud, demanding, and completely obsessed with his mommy. Thankfully, Willow is as laid-back as Luna and she rarely fusses.

"We will finish our cards for Mom," Luna says, looping her arm through Rora's. "And when we come back, they'll be ready for us."

"Go with them," Galen tells Bishop. "And be nice." He drills him with a warning look.

Bishop rolls his eyes. "I always look after my sisters, Daddy. Chill." He slides his arms around his sisters as they retreat to Luna's bedroom to finish drawing their cards. The kids also helped Galen to bake chocolate chip cookies for their mom, and a large batch is presently cooling in the kitchen.

Caz opens the door to Lo's bedroom, and we file into the large master suite. Lo is still asleep, curled on her side in the gigantic bed, the sheets crumpled from our sexual antics last night. It's rare we all sleep in the same bed, but we made an exception last night. Originally, we were considering going away, so we could celebrate Valentine's Day together, but Lo didn't want to leave the kids. Especially Soren, because he's so clingy right now. So, we stayed at home and put the twins in their bedroom, taking the baby monitors into the master suite with us.

"Rise and shine, queenie," Caz says, sitting on the edge of the bed and running his fingers through Lo's hair.

"Hmm," she murmurs, stretching out under the sheets. We all know she's naked under there, and I'm sure my cock isn't the only one hardening.

"We have food." Galen hums, sitting on the other side of Lo, holding the tray carefully on his lap.

"And flowers," Saint adds, jerking his head at Caz. Caz produces the massive bouquet of roses and lilies as Lo pulls herself upright in the bed.

She buries her nose in the petals, inhaling deeply, before setting the vase on her bedside table. "They're gorgeous. Thank you." Stifling a yawn, she smiles at all of us. Her gaze softens when her green eyes land on the twins. "I see you have sleeping babies too."

"They're our favorite kind," Caz jokes.

"You should put them in their cribs," she says, gesturing at me and Saint. The sheet slips down her body, pooling at her waist, and we all drool at the tempting view.

"Damn, queenie." Caz gently cups one of her enlarged

boobs. "I swear these get bigger every time I look at you."

Lo rolls her eyes. "They're full of milk. Of course, they're bigger."

"I'm feeling hungry," Caz quips, waggling his brows.

"Knock that shit off, assface," Saint says, placing Soren down in one of the cribs at the base of the bed. "You're not drinking her breast milk."

This is a running joke, and Caz loves pushing Saint's buttons. Saint is very specific in his views and values, and he takes his role as a father seriously. He is probably the strictest on discipline out of all of us. It's not surprising. He's determined to ensure our kids grow up knowing we love them while understanding they have boundaries too. He wants them to have the kind of structured, loving environment he missed out on.

"I just want a little taste," Caz teases, lowering his mouth toward Lo's left nipple.

Saint yanks him back, pushing him in my direction, as I deposit Willow in her crib. "Have a word with your man."

"Stop winding him up," I murmur, nipping Caz's earlobe with my teeth as I wrap my arm around him from behind.

"It's way too much fun." Caz chuckles.

"You're spoiling me," Lo says, deliberately refocusing the conversation. She holds her arms up as Galen lowers her silk nightgown down over her body.

"You deserve to be spoiled," I say, leaning down to kiss her. "Happy Valentine's, babe."

The others take turns kissing her, and we surround her on the bed as Galen places the tray on her lap.

"You made my favorite omelet." She beams at Galen as she lifts her silverware.

"Mimosas too," Saint adds, distributing the glasses among us. "Because every queen deserves champagne on Valentine's Day."

Keeping a careful watch on the door, we sip our drinks as Lo eats her omelet. It won't be long before the kids descend, and we want to give her her gift first.

"This is for you," Galen says, handing her the small box when she's finished eating. "It's from all of us. We chose it together." Taking the tray, he sets it off to one side.

"I thought we had a rule about no extravagant gifts," she chastises us, narrowing her eyes. Usually, we just exchange cards and she lets us buy her flowers and chocolates, but that's it. The little things matter more to Lo. Like the things we do all year to show her how much we love her. She doesn't want or need materialistic things, and that only makes me love her even more.

"We wanted to make an exception this year," I explain.

"Because our family is complete now," Caz adds, running his fingers up and down her arm.

"And you have made us unbelievably happy," Saint admits, his eyes turning glassy. It's not often Saintly shows emotion, but when he does, it's always centered on Lo and the kids.

"Open it." Galen encourages her, tucking strands of her lavender-streaked hair behind her ear.

Her fingers shake as she pries the box open, and a gasp escapes her lush mouth. "Oh, my God. You guys. This is beautiful," she says, lifting the ring from the cushion.

"It's an eternity ring." Galen helps to slip the platinum band on her finger.

"I love it." Lo holds her hand out, admiring the sparkling diamonds.

We kept it simple. Just a platinum band with a row of fine diamonds.

Her eyes fill with tears as her gaze roams between us. "As I love all of you. I wish I had the words to describe how much you all mean to me. How much I cherish this life we share. I never dared to dream I could be this happy, and it's all thanks to you. You and the kids are my entire world."

"As you are ours." I pull her over onto my lap, and we all wrap our arms around her in a group hug.

"You're stuck with us now," Caz says, pressing a soft kiss to her temple.

"Because we're never letting you go." Saint stares adoringly into her eyes.

Galen plants a tender kiss on her lips. "And we will love you until our dying breaths."

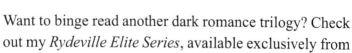

Want to binge read another dark romance trilogy? Check out my *Rydeville Elite Series*, available exclusively from Amazon, in e-book, paperback and audiobook format. *Cruel Intentions* is the first book in the series.

Prefer to read more of my reverse harem romances? Check out my stand-alone, *Surviving Amber Springs*, or my paranormal romance series *Alinthia*!

ABOUT THE AUTHOR

Siobhan Davis is a *USA Today, Wall Street Journal,* and Amazon Top 10 bestselling romance author. **Siobhan** writes emotionally intense stories with swoon-worthy romance, complex characters, and tons of unexpected plot twists and turns that will have you flipping the pages beyond bedtime! She has sold over 1.5 million books, and her titles are translated into several languages.

Prior to becoming a full-time writer, Siobhan forged a successful corporate career in human resource management.

She lives in the Garden County of Ireland with her husband and two sons.

You can connect with Siobhan in the following ways:
Author Website: www.siobhandavis.com
Facebook: AuthorSiobhanDavis
Twitter: @siobhandavis
Instagram: @siobhandavisauthor
Email: siobhan@siobhandavis.com

BOOKS BY SIOBHAN DAVIS

KENNEDY BOYS SERIES

Upper Young Adult/New Adult Contemporary Romance

Finding Kyler

Losing Kyler

Keeping Kyler

The Irish Getaway

Loving Kalvin

Saving Brad

Seducing Kaden

Forgiving Keven

Summer in Nantucket

Releasing Keanu

Adoring Keaton

Reforming Kent

STANDALONES

New Adult Contemporary Romance

Inseparable

Incognito

When Forever Changes

No Feelings Involved

Only Ever You

Second Chances Box Set

Reverse Harem Contemporary Romance

Surviving Amber Springs

Dark Mafia Romance

Condemned to Love

RYDEVILLE ELITE SERIES

Dark High School Romance

Cruel Intentions

Twisted Betrayal

Sweet Retribution

Charlie

Jackson

Sawyer

The Hate I Feel

*Drew^*

THE SAINTHOOD (BOYS OF LOWELL HIGH)

Dark HS Reverse Harem Romance

Resurrection

Rebellion

Reign

True Calling Series Collection

SAVEN SERIES

Young Adult Science Fiction/Paranormal Romance

Saven Deception

Logan

Saven Disclosure

Saven Denial

Saven Defiance

Axton

Saven Deliverance

Saven: The Complete Series

*Coming 2021
^Release date to be confirmed

Visit www.siobhandavis.com for all future release dates. Please note release dates are subject to change based on reader demand and the author's schedule. Subscribing to the author's newsletter or following her on Facebook is the best way to stay updated with planned new releases.

Printed in Great Britain
by Amazon

14886947R00068